THE KINGFISHER TREASURY OF

Irish
Stories

KINGFISHER
a Houghton Mifflin Company imprint
222 Berkeley Street
Boston, Massachusetts 02116
www.houghtonmifflinbooks.com

First published in 1995
2 4 6 8 10 9 7 5 3 1
1TR/0503/THOM/MA/115IWF

LIBRARY OF CONGRESS CATALOGING-IN-PUBLICATION DATA
The Kingfisher treasury of irish stories/[compiled by] James Riordan
[illustrated by] Ian Newsham.—1st American ed.
p. cm.
Summary: A collection of 16 tales, including original stories
by a variety of Irish authors and retellings of traditional folktales.
1. Children's stories, Irish. 2. Tales—Ireland. [1. Ireland—Fiction.
2. Short stories. 3. Folklore—Ireland.]
I. Riordan, James.   II. Newsham, Ian, ill.
PZ5.T754 1995   95-3009
[Fic]—dc20 95-3009   CIP AC

ISBN 0-7534-5672-9

Printed in India

THE KINGFISHER TREASURY OF

Irish Stories

CHOSEN BY JAMES RIORDAN
ILLUSTRATED BY IAN NEWSHAM

KINGFISHER
BOSTON

CONTENTS

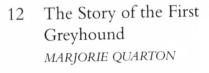

THE MAN WITH NO STORY

Retold by James Riordan

There was a young fellow from this parish long ago, and he used to travel away down the County Limerick, working for the farmers. He would put up here and there along the road. But before long he noticed that he was not so very welcome: people expected him to have the latest news or to keep the night going with a song or a story. Poor Paddy Ahern was heart-scalded, so he was, but what could he do, poor fellow?

Well, one night he was going along a lonely part of the road, and he saw this light in a house away inside the fields; and he made for it. It was a queer, dark, big-looking house, and the door was opened by a queer, dark, big-looking man.

"*O, tar isteach, tá céad fáilte romhat.* Oh, come in, you are a thousand times welcome," says the

7

man. "Take a seat by the fire, Paddy Ahern."

Paddy could not make out how the man knew his name, but he was too afraid to say anything, for it was such a queer place. They had supper, and the man showed Paddy where to sleep. He stretched himself out, tired after the road.

But it was not much rest Paddy got. He was hardly asleep when the door burst open, and in with three men and they dragging a coffin after them. There was no sign of the man of the house.

"Who will help us carry the coffin?" says the first of the men to the other two.

"Who but Paddy Ahern?" says they.

Poor Paddy had to get up and throw on his clothes, though he was shaking with fright. He had to go under the feet of the coffin with one of the men, and the other two went under the head. Off with them out of the door and away across the fields. It was not long before poor Paddy was all wet and dirty from falling into dikes and all torn and bleeding from pulling through hedges and ditches. Every time he stopped they cursed him, and the few times he fell they kicked him until he got up again. Finally, they came to a graveyard, a lonely place with a high wall around it.

"Who will take the coffin over the wall?" says the man.

"Who but Paddy Ahern?" says they.

Poor Paddy had to lift the coffin over the wall, although it very nearly crushed him. He could hardly stand by this time, but they would not let him take a rest.

"Who will dig the grave?" says the first man.

"Who but Paddy Ahern?" says they.

They gave him a spade and a shovel, and made him dig the grave.

"Who will open the coffin?" says the first man.

"Who but Paddy Ahern?" says the other two.

Paddy was nearly fainting with terror, but he had to go down on one knee and take off the screws and lift the lid. And do you know what? The coffin was empty—even though it had been a terrible weight to carry.

"Who will go in the coffin?" asks the first man.

"Who but Paddy Ahern?" says they.

Paddy did not wait for them: away out with him over the wall in one leap, and away across the country, and the three after him with every screech out of them as if it was the hunt.

They nearly had him caught more than once, but he managed to keep in front of them, until he saw a light in a window. He made for it, shouting at the top of his voice for the people of the house to open up and let him in. But who should open the door but the queer, dark, big-looking man? That was too much for Paddy: he fell into the kitchen in a dead faint.

When he came to, it was broad daylight, and the queer man was up and working in the kitchen. There was not a sign of anyone else in the house.

"You are awake, Paddy," says the man of the house. "Did you have a good night's sleep?"

"But I did not," says poor Paddy. "It is exhausted I am after all the hardship I had during the night! And not one single minute longer will I stay in this house, sure I will not!"

He got up and put on his clothes. And would you believe it? There was not a sign of the night's troubles upon them. There were his old working clothes, sure enough, but they were clean and dry. He did not know what to make of it.

"Now listen to me, Paddy Ahern," says the man of the house. "It was how I was sorry for the way you were going along the road, without a story, a song or a handful of riddles in your head. But tell me this much now—haven't you a fine adventure story to be telling in every house you go to after last night?"

Not a word out of Paddy, but to grab up his stick and his bundle and away with him as quick as his legs could carry him. And whatever look he gave back as he crossed the ditch to the main road, there was not a house, nor a sign of one, to be seen—just the bare fields and a few cows grazing.

THE STORY OF THE FIRST GREYHOUND

Marjorie Quarton

Hundreds of years ago, there were no greyhounds in Ireland. Ireland without greyhounds! It was like potatoes without salt, or bacon without cabbage.

There were wolfhounds for hunting the wolf.

Deerhounds for hunting the deer.

Foxhounds for hunting the fox.

Boarhounds for hunting the boar—but there were no greyhounds at all.

The people who lived in Ireland long ago did not realize what they were missing. They had never seen a greyhound, so they could not miss them.

One fine day in harvest time, a rich young man called Terence rode through Nenagh on his way to Dublin. He was guided to the town

12

by the tall keep of the new castle, then he turned westward and crossed the great fair green which gave the town its name. There, he saw some boys cruelly beating a mongrel dog. The dog howled pitifully, and Terence, who had a kind heart, turned his horse and put the boys to flight.

The dog, which stood as high as the sole of Terence's boot as he sat on his horse, was lean, mangy and yellow-eyed. Its legs were long, and so was its tail, which was tucked in against its empty belly.

"Go home," said Terence, for he did not know that the dog had never had a home. He turned his horse's head in the direction of Toomevara and trotted away.

Now Terence was a wealthy young man, and had all he needed in the way of horses, dogs and fine clothes. He loved to dress in bright colors, and it was said by some that he washed himself all over every week. He could not bear any but clean linen next to his skin, and was commonly held by his servants to be mad. Likewise, he would not keep a horse unless it was sound and handsome. It must be free from blemishes and be young and swift.

Terence owned some of the finest deer-hounds in Ireland, and they too were beautiful. They were savage, it is true, with all but Terence, but they were the fastest and hand-somest dogs in the province of Munster. If one of his dogs was mauled in a fight, Terence could not bear to have it near him until its wounds were healed.

As Terence rode down the hill to Roscrea, where he was to change his horse, he chanced to look around, and saw that the dog was following him—the same long-legged mangy cur that he had befriended in Nenagh. Terence turned his horse with the intention of driving it away, but then he thought, it will abandon the chase when I have a fresh horse. Already, it has run seven leagues.

Terence was traveling to Dublin to meet the young lady he was going to marry. Her name was Gráinne, the daughter of a rich merchant, and she was said to be as beautiful as she was wealthy.

The following day, as he rode through Monasterevin, Terence looked around and saw the dog still following; footsore now, and a long way behind. Poor brute, thought Terence, and rode on. By nightfall, the dog was no longer in sight.

It was then, as he crossed the Curragh of Kildare in the twilight that Terence was attacked by bandits. He fought them bravely, but they were many and desperate. They took his horse, and stripped him of his money belt and jewelry. They dared not kill him, for they feared his father's revenge. So they tied his hands and feet, and melted away into the night with his sword, his horse and his purse.

Terence did not know how long he lay in the darkness, with the first frost of autumn chilling him to the bone. He groaned, for the cords that bound his wrists and ankles chafed him sorely.

At length, he felt a warm dampness on his hand and, in the light of early dawn, he saw that the dog was licking blood from his fingers. For many hours it lay by his side, then all of a sudden, it got up and gazed into the distance, its ears lifted. Then it set off at a furious pace, and Terence thought, my last friend has deserted me.

It was not so. The dog had sighted a hare and coursed it until it caught it, killed it and began ravenously to eat it. Then it bethought itself, and began to drag what remained of the carcass toward Terence.

"Thank you, my friend; I haven't come to that," said Terence. "Eat it yourself." The dog did as it was told, and returned to lie beside Terence.

The same day, a band of young men set out from Dublin to meet Terence. They supposed he had lost his way, and they cantered across the Curragh, riding the finest of horses and dressed in their best. They were of the bride's family, and were as fond as Terence of hunting and finery. With them, they had two enormous wolfhounds with jeweled collars.

Terence had fallen into an exhausted sleep, and they might well have failed to see him lying among the gorse bushes had not the dog raised its voice in the most piercing of howls.

In little time, the young men had cut Terence's bonds and heard his story.

"And what is that pray?" asked one of them, pointing a scornful finger at the long-legged dog, crouched shivering, licking its paws.

Terence looked at his friend with new eyes. He looked past the dirty, verminous coat to the faithful heart beneath. What should he say? It was a gray dog, so he said, "He is a greyhound."

"It is the first I have seen, is it a new breed?"

"It is," said Terence. "It is the newest and the rarest breed of all. His name is Finn." With that, he gave his friend the finest name he could think of.

Finn had many sons and daughters and, because there was none like him, they came in many colors. Some were black, some fawn, some brindled, some white.

But the first greyhound was gray.

THE FLYING DISPLAY

Tony Hickey

By three o'clock in the afternoon, the road to the valley was jammed with cars and vans and motor bicycles. A police car blocked the entrance to the valley to prevent anyone from driving in there.

Loudspeakers told the people, who had left their vehicles and walked the last mile or so, to go home.

"There will be no flying display here this afternoon," the voices kept saying. "You are wasting your time. Kindly turn around and go home!"

But, even if anyone felt like heeding this advice, the crowd was now so big that the road was blocked. The twins pointed to the high ground close to the farmhouse. "You'll see better from there," they said.

Everyone was so excited that they did as the twins suggested. No one even asked them what they knew about this flying display. Then the twins found themselves talking to their parents.

"Don't tell me that the two of you are mixed up in all this," said Mr. O'Brien.

"It will be all right, honestly it will," the twins said.

Suddenly there was the sound of loud music from the farmhouse. Granny and Co. had fixed up their own loudspeaker system, which filled the valley with waltz music. The crowd, including Mr. and Mrs. O'Brien, became very quiet. Then in time to the music, Granny Green, with Spit her cat draped around her shoulders, flew up over the clump of trees.

Then came Mrs. Fitzgerald and Mr. Grogan and Miss Lynch. Then came the rest of the elderly people.

The watching crowd gasped and applauded and cried out in amazement as Granny and Co. swooped and circled and turned, always in time to the music. Then as the music came to an end, the flyers gracefully descended out of sight

behind the trees.

The crowd went wild. None of them had ever imagined, much less seen, anything like the flying display. Dozens of people surged forward toward the farmhouse.

Granny Green's voice came over the loudspeakers. "Please don't trample any more than is necessary on the grass or frighten the sheep. Please go back to Dara. We will come and explain everything to you as soon as you have taken all your cars and vans and motor bicycles home."

The crowd was so impressed by the firmness of Granny's voice and so anxious to hear the full story that immediately people began to leave the valley. Soon there were only Mr. and Mrs. O'Brien and the twins left.

Granny Green came out from among the trees and hurried toward them. "I'm sorry I couldn't let you into the secret sooner," she said to Mr. and Mrs. O'Brien. "But if you will give me a lift back to Dara, I will explain everything to you."

When Granny did explain, Mr. and Mrs. O'Brien were as amazed as the twins had been. So too were the people gathered around the hotel. Television crews had by now turned up with their cameras, as had many reporters from the national newspapers and radio stations.

Within hours, there were special editions of the evening newspapers on the city streets with headlines like:

GRANNY GREEN TAKES TO THE SKIES!

A NEW AGE DAWNS FOR OUR SENIOR CITIZENS!

SPIT GETS A BIRD'S-EYE VIEW OF THE WORLD!

Granny Green and her friends had become the most famous people not just in Ireland but in the whole world! There was even talk of setting up flying schools for the elderly wherever they were needed!

"I just hope that it will work as well for people elsewhere as it did for us in the valley," Granny Green said as she got ready to leave the hotel where she had spent the last three nights with the O'Briens.

"Of course it'll work," said Mrs. O'Brien.

"And don't forget that you said that we could try to fly as well," said the twins.

"Now hold on just a second," said Mrs. O'Brien. "I'm not sure that it is a very good thing for people of your age to be able to fly."

"Maybe that's what Granny Green meant when she said that it might not work for everyone," sighed the twins. "We will just have to wait and see," said Granny Green. "Now where has Spit got to?"

"Miaow!" said Spit.

Granny Green and the O'Briens looked up. There, high above the entrance to the hotel, was the black cat, turning and miaowing and spitting with delight.

"Oh, you clever cat!" Granny Green cried. "You can fly all by yourself!"

"Of course I can," said Spit.

"And talk! He can really talk! We thought that we had imagined it the other day!" laughed the twins. "If Spit can learn both those things, surely we can learn to fly! We'd be very careful!"

"Well, we'll see," said their parents.

"Yes, we'll see," agreed Granny Green.

Then she took a few steps backward, ran a few steps forward and off she went, up in the air.

"'Bye!" yelled the O'Briens.

"'Bye!" Granny and Spit replied. Then they flew off across the town of Dara and back to Granny's little house at the entrance to the Valley of the Crows.

THE LEPRECHAUN

Edna O'Brien

Bridget was sent out as usual to fetch a bucket of water but when she got to the well near the house she found it had dried up so she had to go across some fields to another well that was near an old disused monastery. Now as she was walking along she suddenly heard tap tap, tap tap, and she stopped and thought to herself "could it be," because Bridget like every other girl knew that the little fairy cobbler came up from underground and mended shoes. But not only that, but that the leprechaun had the power of bestowing wealth on anyone who caught him and who kept him in their sight.

"Oh," said Bridget to herself, "this is my chance to be a rich woman."

So she put the bucket down and she went in

near the hedge and she crept along until she caught sight of him. Quite a beau he was in his red coat laced with gold and cocked hat with a green feather, an apron over his knees and he hammering away at a little silver dance shoe. Beside him was a little vessel full of drink. So up she came behind him and she seized hold of the back of his coat with the command, "Deliver or die."

"Oh moidy," says he in a squeaky voice, "a highwayman."

"Wirra man," said Bridget. "I'm just a young girl."

"You're hurting me," said the leprechaun and he tried to wriggle out but of course she had a tight hold of him and informed him that she had no intention of letting him go until he told her where the crock of gold was hidden.

"I don't know," he whimpered.

"You sly boots," said Bridget and she squeezed harder.

"Such a purty colleen ketchin' a body as if he was a robber."

"If you don't tell me I'll cut the head off you," said Bridget.

"What wrong did I do to be thrated like this?"

"No wrong yet," said Bridget, inquiring what was in the vessel.

"Beer," said the leprechaun, "strong beer."

"Did you steal it from a house?" said Bridget.

"I brewed it," said he and boasted that he learned brewing off a Dane.

"In that case, you know where the crock of gold is," she said. "You're a smart sprite."

"I'm a poor cobbler," he protested.

Bridget threatened to carry him into the village and to plonk him down on the big weighing scales in the marketplace where the entire town would see him and where he would first be cross-examined and then squeezed like a sausage by stronger men than her.

"I'm bested, I'm bested," he said.

"You are," said Bridget. "So you might as well get down to business."

"Who'd think it, a nice girl like you," said he.

"Give over your *plamais*," said Bridget, "and bring me to where the loot is."

"We have a bit of a walk," said he. Then he asked to be let down. But Bridget was taking no chances; she picked him up in her arms and she carried him like a baby.

"It's desmasculating," he said, kicking and yelping, but Bridget gave him a few clouts and threatened to dump him in the well if he didn't

behave himself.

They crossed a field and climbed over a gate, then into a paddock, past the lime kiln and over a ditch into a huge field that was covered in ragwort. It stretched from one end to another, great high stalks of yellow ragwort.

"Let me down," said the leprechaun.

Bridget let him down but made sure to keep a good hold on him in case he disappeared. They began to wade their way into the middle of the field and every so often he put his ear to the root of a stalk to "reconnoitre" as he put it.

"It's under here," said the leprechaun, "dig there and you'll get your guineas."

"Dig!" Bridget exclaimed in a huff. She had expected to pull the stalks up and find the booty—she was not in the mood for digging.

"You'll have to dig deep," said the leprechaun, "ten feet or maybe more."

"With what? My hands!"

"With a spade," said the leprechaun, a bit saucily.

Bridget wanted him to accompany her back to the farm to get the spade but he convinced her that that was a mistake. He said that he had to keep an eye on the stalk in case another leprechaun came, because they were avaricious, like humans, and they were bound to be passing by as day began, and they betook themselves to the burrows and chambers that led to their secret abodes.

"They wouldn't trick *you*," she said.

"Oh, they would, they're all thieves," he said.

"Suppose you do a disappearing act," cautioned Bridget.

"I'll tell you what," said the leprechaun, "I'll put a garter around it and you'll recognize it even if I'm not here."

"Right," said Bridget.

He slipped off a tiny little red garter that was keeping up his wool sock and hung it over the piece of ragwort.

Bridget ran for dear life. She crossed the fields, she passed the ruin, she took the stepping-stones over the stream and went directly to the farmyard where shovels and implements were kept.

Back she was, panting but delighted at her speed. However, a nasty shock was in store for her: what did she see but a red garter on every single stalk of ragwort and no sign of Mr. Slimy Leprechaun.

"Oh thunder and sparables," she cried and she started to dig. Well, she dug and she dug and she dug and all she found was clay with worms and maggots in it, and she swore by the vestments that if ever she caught that bucko she'd squeeze him into putty, but she never did find him and the chances are she never will.

plamais = sweet talk

PETIE FLIMIN AND THE WHALE

Eamon Kelly

A Killarney man working in Kildare one time was very taken by the fine land that's there, stretching away as far as the eye can see.

"I'll bet you now," says his boss to him one day, "ye haven't so much land in Kerry."

"Bedad," says the workman, "we haven't so, but something else, let me tell you," says he, "we have so much land in Kerry that we had to pile it up in heaps!" A thing that was true for him. Look at Macgillycuddy's Reeks! And Corrán Tuathail, the highest peak in Ireland. And the Purple Mountain, and Torc, and Stoompa, and Crohane, not to mention Mangerton, where my story begins.

Now, it is said that there was a volcano on the top of Mangerton in ancient times—we're only going by what we hear. And when this volcano

31

burned itself out—maybe the rain quenched it—the crater, as it is called, filled up and became a lake. It is there to be seen today by anyone that will go to the trouble to climb the hill. A black lake in a black hollow, and it is known as the Devil's Punch Bowl, and there's no bottom to it. And how was that found out? Simple.

One fine summer's day a man, and a local man too, his name was Petie Flimin, was at the top of Mangerton. The day was very hot, so he took off his overcoat. The ground was rough, and as he walked along he lost his footing and fell into the Punch Bowl. Down he went, but he didn't come up.

His overcoat was found there by his people, and he was given over for dead. He was prayed for, and there was crying and lamentation; but great indeed was his mother's surprise, for what happened a couple of days after only that she got a telegram from Australia asking her to send him a change of clothes! This was his way of saying that he was safe and sound.

And wasn't that the quickest trip anyone ever made to Australia! It would take a couple of months at that time to get there by ship, not to mind the expense.

He worked away in Sydney for a couple of years and then came home. A fine man he was, with a huge wideawake hat that he never took off only when he was going in to Mass.

He wasn't too long at home when the notion rose in his head to see more of the world. And where did he hit for this time but Wales. He went over by ship from Cork to Fishguard, and a dangerous undertaking it was too, the year being 1914, when England and Germany were at war. However, he arrived in Wales all in one piece, and he worked away there making big money. I don't know what job he had. I think I heard he was a stonemason.

While he was in Wales he got a letter from his mother telling him to go up to London to see his Uncle Jer. She forgot to mention any street or any avenue, or she didn't give him any number of anything else, only "Go up to London." That is what she said! He went up. Now, as we all know, London is a fairly big place, and he didn't meet his Uncle Jer. He called to the Crown in Cricklewood, and to Crowns besides, where Irish people were likely to assemble, but there was no sign of his uncle. And of course his money was going, burning a hole in his pocket until 'twas spent.

And finally this evening he was down to his last shilling. He bought a loaf of bread with that, and he was going along by the edge of a park looking for some likely place for a night's shelter, seeing he hadn't the price of his lodgings. He came to this big sloping object with a mouth on it as wide as a barrel. He climbed in and let his legs skate down before him till they came to the bottom. Well, he was out of view, so he made himself comfortable and dozed off to sleep in his great big hat.

Now, if Petie Flimin was in any way acquainted with artillery, a thing he wasn't, he would know that he was inside in the barrel of a big gun, an eighteen-pounder.

Came the morning, and what happened but a squad of military came marching out and two officers in charge of them. "Do you know," says one officer, "I think this would be a right good morning to have a shot at the enemy."

"You're right," says the second one. "It might be raining tomorrow—Sergeant," says he, "is that gun loaded?"

"It is," says the sergeant, "and well loaded."

"Look smart so," says the officer, "and put a match to the fuse."

The sergeant put a match to the fuse, and the flame ran up along it. Well, there was an almighty explosion, and when Petie Flimin woke up he was well on his way to the continent of Europe, holding onto his huge hat! But whatever was wrong with the Englishman's aim, he was away wide of the mark. Where did Petie Flimin land but in a field in France, a meadow by the river that was under hay, and the hay was cut and made up in big haycocks.

Petie picked himself up, and then he heard all the tatter-ra-ra-ra, rifle fire—such commotion! And not wanting in any way to become involved in this carry-on, Petie climbed up on a cock of hay and dug himself down into the middle of it and fluffed up the hay all around him, so that it would be the clever detective that'd make him out there. He even managed to cover his enormous hat!

He had the loaf of bread all the time, so he settled into eating it and finished the last crumb. When evening came he nodded off. I suppose with the excitement of the journey over and everything he was tired out, poor man, and in no time at all he was in dreamland.

It was just as well, for that night the heavens opened, a pure deluge, and when Petie Flimin woke up in the morning he was sailing down the river inside in the cock of hay. Down he went, past village and town, pier, port, and harbor, till he found himself outside in the broad expanse of the Atlantic Ocean.

The day turned out fine, as often happens after a night's rain, and Petie Flimin took off his shirt and began waving it as he stood on top of the cock of hay, thinking to attract a ship.

He didn't know what was before him. It

wasn't a ship he attracted but something else. What should he see making for him but a huge whale, with his mouth opened back to his ears: and before Petie Flimin had time to bless himself he was gone down into the inside of the whale, cock of hay and all!

Dia linn tonight, the poor man, there he was! He got out of the gun, but how was he going to get out of this! It was dark inside the whale. Where was the illumination to come from? And to calm his nerves Petie took out his pipe and cracked a match to redden it, and there he saw every sort of fish that was ever seen or imagined, and they all churning around looking for a way out. With that a thought struck him, and what did he do? He put the match to the cock of hay, and damp and all as it was, it lit.

"What's this?" says the whale when the flames began to tickle his insides. "What's this?" You know, he had a feeling like he was getting an awful lot of heartburn, as if something he had eaten didn't agree with him. "Oh, *a Dhiabhall*," says he, "I won't be able to stand this much longer."

And the whale settled himself for a big blow,

and he blew, and he blew, and he blew Petie
Flimin, cock of hay, fire, flames and ashes so
high into the heavens that Petie thought the
sun was coming to meet him. Up he went and
the cock of hay blazing behind him. That'd be
the day to have the spyglasses. And wasn't it the
mercy of goodness that the man didn't go into
orbit!

While he was above, the world was turning
under him, which was all to the good, as we'll
see further on. When he began to fall he fell
with such speed that he said to himself, "If I hit
the ground at this rate I'll go down through it
like a knife through butter on a hot flag."

And wasn't it great presence of mind for him
to think of holding his hat over him like an
umbrella. It acted as a brake, and he floated

down and landed in the field in front of his own
house, without hurt or injury. He was the first
man I ever heard of to come home from
England without paying his fare!

Sin é mo scéal anois daoibh. Sin a bhfuil. That's
my story now for you. That's all there is.

Dia linn = God be with us.
a Dhiabhall = the Devil

NEILLY AND THE FIR-TREE

John O'Connor

Neilly watched dreamily as the boy in the red jersey dropped from the big fir-tree back on to the ground again. The rest of the boys gathered around calling out questions, but Neilly didn't move. He stood with his hands behind his back, a look of sadness in his large hazel eyes.

The boy in the red jersey shook his head, obviously very thankful to be back on firm ground again.

"It's no good! Nobody'll ever be able to climb that tree."

He was the third to have attempted it. Two of the others had already tried, but they also had failed. The boy in the red jersey had the name of being the best climber of them all, and now that the big fir-tree had beaten him too, well it didn't seem much good for anyone else to try.

He shook his head again. "Nobody'll ever be able to climb that tree . . . You might be able to get *past* that part all right, but you'd never be able to get back down again. You'd be stuck there all night. Isn't that right Franky?"

All the boys walked backward out into the field, staring upward, until halfway up the tree, they could see the bare part like a faint magic girdle encircling the trunk. Here for a space of about six or seven feet the trunk was devoid of any branches. The boys argued and shook their heads. No one took the slightest notice of little Neilly standing a few yards away.

There were three firs standing on top of the hill. Like three monuments erected by some long-vanished race, they towered up into the air, a landmark for miles around.

Neilly gave a faint shudder as he looked up into the fir. He felt so terribly small and insignificant beside this glowering monster. Neilly was a small slight lad of about nine. He was easily the youngest and smallest of the entire group. His legs and arms were slender as reeds, and he wore a pair of ponderous looking black boots—no stockings. His right boot was soaking wet, and smeared with pale, gluey mud.

That was where he had nearly fallen into St. Bridget's drain, about ten minutes ago. Everyone else had jumped it except him. Poor Neilly! How he wished he were a bit bigger, so that he could jump and climb as well as the other lads. It wasn't his fault that he was so small, but the rest of the boys didn't think of that. When they did anything that he couldn't, they just jeered at him, or worse even— ignored him altogether. Neilly suddenly became aware of his companions glances.

The boy in the red jersey was pointing at him dramatically.

"There you are!" he shouted. "I bet you Neilly could climb it though. Couldn't you Neilly?"

"Ah, he can't even jump St. Bridget's drain, yet, even," another boy chimed in. At this Neilly bit his lip, hiding his wet, muddy boot behind his dry left one.

The boys came closer.

"Ah, poor wee Neilly! What are you blushing about Neilly? What are you blushing about?"

The boy in the red jersey stuck his hands up.

"I still say that Neilly could climb that tree." He put his hand on Neilly's shoulder. "Couldn't you, Neilly?"

Neilly shook the hand off instantly. The boy gave him a push, and then the rest of the boys began pushing him too. Neilly became infuriated.

He made a wild swing with his boot, but the boys only jeered louder. Neilly's rage increased. He broke through his tormentors, and rushed over to the fir.

"For two pins I would climb your ould tree for you," he raged. "Do you think I couldn't, like?"

The jeering grew louder. The boys were enjoying themselves immensely. With a mighty effort Neilly forced himself to be calm. He turned to the tree. The lower part of the enormous trunk was worn smooth and shiny, where the cows had come to scratch. Neilly stripped off his boots, then, standing on a great, humpbacked root, he gave a great jump, reaching for a huge rusty staple which was driven into the trunk about five feet off the ground. He caught it, skinning his knee against the bark. He made another lunge toward the first branch a little higher, and drew himself up, casting a swift, triumphant glance at the boys below.

As he climbed he became filled with joy. The rich spicy scent of resin hung in the air like incense, and his hands and feet grew rough and sticky, which, of course, made his progress all the more easy.

Now and then he glanced through the heavy green foliage. The fields seemed a great distance below, but the thrill he felt was one of daring

rather than fear. He could hear the
faint sound of his name being
called by the boys below. But
he urged on, too excited to answer.

He came at last to the bare part,
and here, craning up, he caught
his breath in dismay. Except for
a few withered branches, the
column of the tree was bare
indeed. Above, near enough
to mock him, but far
enough to frighten him,
the heavy growth of the
tree resumed.

In some past
storm perhaps, a
saber of lightning
had put its brand

here, killing the branches but leaving the bole itself unharmed.

With a sinking heart Neilly circled the tree, searching for a reliable grip, but there was nothing except those few, puny branches, and they looked too frail to bear even his weight.

It would be terrible to have to turn back now. For a moment he felt like risking all in one mad hopeless leap for the foliage above. Then a look of fierce determination settled on his face.

One of the stricken branches grew just within reach of his fingers. He gripped it cautiously, as near to the trunk as possible. He pressed gingerly and it gave a few ominous creaks. The pounding of his heart increased. Gradually he pulled at the branch until at last his entire weight was drooping from it. Hardly daring to breathe, he prized himself up inch by inch, and then grabbed frantically at another branch higher up. He closed his eyes fully expecting it to snap, but although it gave a loud, terrifying creak and shivered alarmingly, it held. Panting, he struggled up until he was able to stand on the bottom branch.

For a minute he hugged the trunk afraid to move another inch. The rough, scenty bole of the fir, seemed the most beautiful thing in the world. Then, fearfully, he allowed his eyes to

creep upward. Tremblingly, he reached up with his right hand, scraping it over the bark, but six inches separated his fingers from the lowermost living branch. He glanced down at the rotten branch he was standing on, and his head began to spin. For a time he stood pressed against the trunk, groaning softly to himself.

Then he looked up and reached his hand out

again. He eased himself gently away from the trunk, keeping his eyes fixed as though by hypnotism on the branch above. The tip of his tongue stuck out. His legs bent slightly. Then he *sprang*.

With a loud crack, the branch below him broke off, but at the same time the fingers of his right hand closed over the one above, and he hung, swinging wildly. He brought his left hand up, gave himself a few twisting heaves, and then he was sitting safely on the branch, panting like an exhausted runner.

He got up at last and climbed on up the trunk that was tapering now. He climbed fast and impatiently as though he were being pursued by someone, and at last he came to the very top.

He stood spellbound, with the tiny green world stretched beneath, like a view from a picture book. The cows and the sheep in the far-off fields looked like tiny plasticine toys. A small cold breeze probed through his jersey making him shiver and the three swayed gently, sending a quaint thrill through his stomach. Below him, down the great spine of fir, the pale brown branches jutted out like a framework of bones.

Neilly shouted, calling the names of the boys below, and soon he saw them, running like little

gnomes over the field, and down the hill. He had to laugh at them. He could hear their thin excited chatter, as they pointed upward, shading their eyes. Neilly hung there enraptured. His heart swelled and the keen fresh air stung the inside of his nostrils, making his eyes swim. Then at last he gave the boys one last wave and started down again. The boys still stood below pointing upward engrossed in his descent.

When he reached the bare part again he sat on a branch, and swung his legs. He felt very calm, as though he were only stopping for a rest. Then gradually he became uneasy. He stood, rubbing his wrist over his lips, and glancing this way and that. Far, far below, so far that he now shuddered, he could see the boys still hunched together, pointing. He could hear their shouts, tiny pinpoints of sound. "Ah he's stuck now. He'll never get down now . . ."

Neilly circled the tree, searching for a

toehold, but the only one had vanished, when that dead branch had snapped beneath him. Hardly knowing what he was doing, he swung out on a branch and hung down weaving to and fro. He looked down along his chest beyond his twisting legs, feasting his eyes on the branches below. His feet clawed out, trying to grasp at them. Suddenly there was a crack and the branch broke! He gave a terrified cry, and his body dropped like a plummet.

With a shock that jarred his whole body, both his feet struck a branch directly underneath. He sagged forward, but at the same moment, his out-thrust hands closed over another branch above him, blocking his headlong fall. He hung for a moment, stretched between the two branches, in a kind of daze.

Then in a little while he recovered, and began to clamber on down. Once he missed his foothold, and almost fell again. He felt a streak of pain along the inside of his leg, above the knee, as a ragged twig tore the skin. But he continued on his way.

Gradually his strength and courage returned, and when he at last dropped back on to solid earth, he was smiling, and his eyes shone. The instant he hit the ground again, the boys swarmed around, cheering and clapping him on the back. Neilly retreated a few steps breathlessly.

"Good man, Neilly!" the boy in the red jersey was shouting. "You did what nobody else here the day would have done. Boy-oh-boy when we seen you dropping down that bare part there, we sure thought you were a goner. Didn't we boys?"

"We sure did!" the rest of the boys chorused. "That was powerful, Neilly."

"Dropping down?" Neilly thought. "Dropping down?" He opened his mouth to say, "but the branch broke. I didn't drop. I fell!"

Then he stopped. If they thought he had dropped it, let them. He *would* have dropped it anyway, if the branch he was standing on hadn't broken off first and foremost. Of course he would! He would have dropped it like anything!

Anyway, fall or drop, he had climbed the tree, and that's what nobody else had done. Ha, he'd shown them, so he had! They wouldn't jeer at him now! It wouldn't be "poor wee Neilly" anymore now . . .

The boys brought his boots over for him, and the boy in the red jersey cleaned his muddy one with grass.

As Neilly was sitting down putting on his boots, his trousers slipped up, and he was surprised to see a long red scratch on his leg. Then he remembered where he had slipped on his downward journey.

The boys all bent down to examine the wound, and then they began advising him to come home, and get some iodine on it. Neilly smiled. It was only a scratch really, and not painful at all, but for some reason he felt terribly proud of it.

As the boys escorted him over the fields, home, he put on a slight limp, and every twenty yards or so, he would glance back at the middle fir that he'd climbed, and then down at his leg again, and then back to the fir again, and his eyes were shining with wonder and joy.

UNA AND THE GIANT CUCULLIN

Retold by James Riordan

Of all the giants that ever walked the vales of
Erin, the giant Cucullin was the strongest.
With a blow of his mighty fist he could squash a
mountain into a cowpat, and he would go about
the land with one such cowpat in his pouch to
scare the other giants.

He scared them all right. They tried to keep
out of his way, but he hunted them down,
one by one, and beat the living daylights out
of them; then they scampered off into the
mountains to lick their wounds.

There was one giant, though, that Cucullin
had not yet thrashed, and that was Finn Mac
Cool. The reason was simple: Finn Mac Cool
was so afraid of Cucullin that he kept well out of
his way. He even built his house on the top of a
windy mountain to keep a lookout all around

him; and whenever the mighty giant appeared in the distance, Finn was off like a shot from a cannon, hiding in bush or bog or barrow.

But Finn could not keep his foe at bay forever. And Cucullin had vowed he would not rest until he had flattened the cowardly Finn. Finn knew the day must come. He knew that by sucking his thumb: that made all things clear to him and he could peer into the future.

So there he was, this Finn, sitting outside his house upon the bleak, windy mountain, sucking his great thumb. Suddenly, he upped and rushed into the house, shaking like a leaf and crying to his wife Una:

"Cucullin is coming this way. This time there's no escape; my thumb tells me so!"

"What time is he due?" asks Una calmly.

Finn sucked his thumb again.

"At three o'clock this afternoon. He means to squash me flat and carry me in his pouch along with his cowpat!"

"Oh does he?" says Una. "Now leave things

to me. Haven't I pulled you out of the mire many times before?"

"That you have," says Finn, and he stopped his shivering.

Una now went down to three friends at the foot of the mountain, and at each house she borrowed an iron griddle.

Once home with her griddles, she baked half a dozen cakes, each as big as a basket; and inside three she put an iron griddle while the dough was soft. Then she placed the cakes in a row upon two shelves: three above, three below, so that she would know which one was which.

At two o'clock she glanced out of the window and spied a speck upon the horizon; she guessed it was Cucullin himself coming. Straightaway, she dressed Finn in nightgown and cap, and tucked him into a wicker cradle.

"Now, Finn," she says, "you'll be your own baby. Lie still and leave it to me. Suck your thumb so as you'll know what I want you to do."

Finn did as he was told.

"Oh and by the way," says Una, "where does that bully of a giant keep all his strength?"

Finn stuck his thumb in his mouth and said, "His strength is in the middle finger of his right hand. Without that finger he'd be as weak as a baby."

With that they sat waiting for himself to appear. And it was not long before a giant fist pounded on the door.

Finn screwed his eyes shut, drew the blanket up around his nose and tried to keep his teeth from chattering. Boldly Una flung open the door—and there stood the mighty Cucullin.

"Is this the house of Finn Mac Cool?" asks he.

"The very one," says Una. "Come yourself in and sit yourself down."

Cucullin took a seat and stared about him.

"That's a bonny-looking baby you have there, Mrs. Mac Cool," says he. "Would his father be at home, I wonder?"

"Faith and he's not," says she. "He went tearing down the mountain a few hours ago, saying he was out to catch some pipsqueak called Cucullin. Heaven help the poor man when my Finn lays his hands on him; there won't be a hair or toenail of him left."

"I am Cucullin himself, Mrs. Mac Cool," says the visitor. "I've been on your husband's track this past year or more. Yet he's always hiding from me; for sure he can't be so very big and strong?"

"*You* are Cucullin!" exclaims Una in a scornful voice. "Did you ever see my Finn?"

"Well, no. How could I? He always gives me the slip."

"Gives you the slip!" says she. "Gives you the thrashing of your life, more likely. I mean you no ill, sir, but if you take my advice you'll steer well clear of him. He's as hard as rock and swift as the wind. Which reminds me: would you do me a favor and turn the house around, the wind is on the turn."

"*Turn the house around?*" muttered Cucullin.

"For sure," says Una. "That's what Finn does when the wind is in the east."

Cucullin stood up and went outside. He crooked the middle finger of his right hand three times, seized the house in his arms and turned it back to front.

When Finn felt the house turn around, he pulled the blanket over his head and his teeth chattered all the more.

But Una just nodded her thanks as if it were quite

natural, then asked another favor.

"With all this dry weather we're having," says she, "I'm clean out of water. Can you fill this jug for me?"

"And where will I fill it?" asks Cucullin.

"Do you see that big rock on top of yonder hill? When we need water Finn lifts the rock and takes water from the spring beneath. Just as soon as you fetch some water we'll have a nice cup of tea."

With a frown, Cucullin took the jug and walked down the mountain and up yonder hill. When he reached the rock, he scratched his head in wonder: it was at least as tall as himself, and twice as wide. He held up his right hand, crooked the middle finger nine times, then took the rock in his brawny arms and heaved. With a mighty effort he tore the rock out of the ground, and four hundred feet of solid rock below as well. And out gushed a stream that gurgled and roared down the hillside so loudly it made Finn shut his ears with both hands.

"Dear wife," he cried, "if that giant lays his

hands on me, he'll crush every bone in my body."

"He has to find you first," says Una.

She greeted the jug-bearer with a smile of thanks as he came through the door.

"Now take a seat while I put the kettle on."

As soon as the tea was poured, Una set three cakes before Cucullin—the ones with iron griddles in them. Now all that hard work had made Cucullin hungry. Smacking his lips, he picked up a cake and took a great bite of it. Oh dear! With a wild yell, he spat out the cake and his two front teeth as well.

"What sort of cake is this? It's as hard as nails!"

"That's Finn's favorite," says Una. "He's mighty partial to it; so is the baby in the cradle. Perhaps it's too hard-baked for a weakling like you. Here, try this one, it's a mite softer than the first."

It certainly smelled good. This time he took an even bigger bite. But, oh dear! Again he spat it out along with two more teeth.

"You can keep your cakes," he shouted, "or I'll have no gnashers left."

"God bless us," exclaims Una. "There's no need to shout so loud and wake the baby. It's not my fault your jaws are weak."

Now, just at that moment Finn sucked his

thumb and guessed what Una wanted him to do. Opening his mouth he let out the greatest, rip-roaring yell he'd ever made.

"Yooowwwllllllllllllll!"

"Well, bejaysus," spluttered Cucullin. "What a pair of tonsils that baby's got! Does it take after its father?"

"When his father gives a shout," says Una, "you can hear him from here to Tipperary!"

Cucullin was beginning to feel uneasy. Glancing nervously toward the cradle, he saw the child was sucking its thumb again.

"He'll be crying for some cake any minute now," says Una. "It's his feeding time."

At once Finn began to howl:

"CAAA-AAKKKE!"

"Put that in your mouth," says she. And she handed Finn a cake from the top shelf.

After eating every crumb, Finn roared out again.

"CAAA-AAKKKE!"

When the baby was well into this third cake, Cucullin got up to go.

"I'm off now, Mrs. Mac Cool," says he. "If that baby is anything like its father, Finn'll be more than a match for me. 'Tis a bonny baby you have there, missus."

"If you're so fond of babies, come and take a closer look at the little laddie," says she.

Taking Cucullin by the arm, she guided him to the cradle.

"The baby's teeth are coming through well," says Una. "Take a feel of them."

Thinking to please the woman before making his escape, Cucullin put his fingers into the baby's mouth to feel its teeth.

Can you guess what happened?

When he pulled his fingers out, there were only four remaining: his middle finger had been bitten off.

You could have heard the yell from there to Spain!

Now that his strength was gone, the once mighty Cucullin began to grow smaller and smaller, until he was no bigger than one of the cakes. High above him, Una and Finn Mac Cool laughed and mocked the little man. The tiny figure tottered out of the house and down the mountain, fleeing for dear life.

He was never again seen in Erin.

As for Finn, he was ever grateful for the brains of his dear wife Una.

THE FOUR MAGPIES

Sigerson Clifford

When the big foxy cat saw the donkey and cart outside the door and old Tim reddening his pipe for the road he knew his master was going to the village and he'd be alone until nightfall. When the mood took himself he slipped away from the house for the length of a week without as much as by-your-leave but he kicked up an almighty fuss whenever Tim left him alone for even half a day.

After the fashion of people who live by themselves in lonely places Tim always talked to his cat as if he was human.

"I'll be back before dark, I tell you, and I'll buy a few mackerel for you from Seamuseen O. Will that satisfy you, now?"

The cat steered the schooner-mast of his tail between Tim's legs and meowed fiercely.

" 'Tisn't that you deserve mackerel, you lazy
scoundrel. The house ate with mice and you're
doing nothing about it. I declare to Jericho if
the mice formed a pipers' band you'd march at
the head of it carrying the banner instead of
gobbling them up, whatever seed or breed of
cats you're sprung from, you scamp."

The cat followed Tim to where the boreen
melted into the grandeur of the main road, and
perched on the fence looking after him and
crying as though he smelled the
end of the world coming across
the mountain. He stood there
wailing until the cart rattled
around a bend in the road
and then curled up under a
furze bush and fell asleep.

Beyond the Three Eye Bridge, Tim heard a chuckle in the air and looked up. It was a magpie making a movable black and white patch on the tent of the sky.

"One for luck," said Tim. "That's a good start to the day anyhow."

A second magpie leaped up from the field behind the river and climbed to meet the first.

"Two for joy," said old Tim, "that's better again, faith."

Half a mile further on in the Dean's field he saw a third magpie perched on a cow's back like a cheeky jockey.

"Three to get married," quoted Tim. "What do you think of that for advice, Barney?"

The donkey threw up his head meaning to say they were better off as they were with no woman flinging orders about like oats to goslings.

"Begor," said Tim, "there's no sense in tackling at seventy-five what you were afraid of at twenty-one. Three to get married, fine girl you are!"

The words of an old ballad, about a damsel who lived on the mountains and whose stockings were white, ran into his mind and he began to sing them softly to shorten the journey. At the outskirts of the village he saw Razor Sullivan's small son, Daneen, standing

beside the gate.

"Hello Tim," the boy said, "I'll give you three guesses as to what I have behind my back."

Tim halted the donkey, pursed his lips, and wrinkled his forehead to add importance to the occasion.

"Is it Finn Mac Cool's magic razor that was sharp enough to shave a mouse asleep?"

"No, no," cried Daneen with delight. "Guess again, Tim."

"Is it the eye of the King of the Fomoricans that could see around corners?"

"You're miles out, Tim. Guess again."

"Then it must be the golden angel that flew off with the Rock of Cashel last week."

The boy whooped with delight at his victory,

and showed him the young magpie he had hidden behind his back.

"I found him in the wood and I'm going to make a pet of him and, maybe, teach him to talk," said the boy.

The magpie said nothing but eyed Tim as though he was measuring him for a coffin.

The old man drove into the village, the jingle about the magpies nagging at his brain. Four to die, the last line ran of it. He felt as healthy as a herring, but then it wasn't the sick ones who went all the time. Patch Fitzmaurice saw four magpies before he died a year ago and he was never a day sick in his life.

By the time he drew level with the chapel he decided to make his will without further delay. The village was too small to support a solicitor but Patrick Monaghan who kept the hardware shop would oblige him. He tied the donkey to the pole outside the window, went in and whispered his business to Monaghan who sat him in the parlor while he fetched pen and paper.

"I'll have to make my mark, Mr. Monaghan, for I can't read or write. My father, God rest him, didn't trouble to make a scholar out of me," said Tim.

Mr. Monaghan smiled under his foxy mustache and filled his fountain pen.

"Education can have its drawbacks, too,

Tim," he replied. He didn't say what the draw-backs were.

The will was a simple matter. Tim had £500 in the Post Office, one acre of land, a house and a cat. With the exception of £20 for Masses he left everything to his favorite niece, Abigail Falvey, on condition that she looked after his cat. The will was witnessed by Monaghan's two servant-girls. Tim gave him a pound for his trouble and went out to his donkey.

Further up the street he ran into his neighbor, James Donnelly. James had a scowl on his face that stretched from the peak of his cap to the knot of his tie.

"What's worrying you now, James?" he asked.

"It's my Aunt Mary's will," replied Donnelly.

"There's going to be law over it and by the time we're through with the courts there won't be a shilling in the kitty. That eegit, Monaghan,

67

made a mess of the will when he was drawing it up."

"Did he, faith!" said Tim, trying to look unconcerned.

When James was gone he sat in the cart thinking about his own will and wondering what he should do. He saw Father O'Carroll going in the chapel gate and he hurried after him. He took the will from his pocket and handed it to him.

"It's my will, Father. I'd be deeply obliged if you'd take a look at it and see if 'tis in order. You see, I can't read or write."

Father O'Carroll read the will.

"Yes, it seems to be quite in order. You've left everything to your niece, Abigail Falvey, With the exception of £20 for Masses and £50 to your good friend, Patrick Monaghan."

Tim thanked him and took back the will. As

he walked toward the street he tore it into little pieces and made a ball of it in the heel of his fist. He returned to Monaghan's shop and went in the door. Monaghan came to serve him with a £50 smile under his mustache.

"I've run short of money," Tim explained, "and I was wondering if you could lend me a pound until the next time I'm in the village."

"Certainly, Tim, and ten of them," said Monaghan.

"One will do," Tim told him. "I hate owing too much money."

He went out the door and didn't bother to look back.

BIDDY'S BIRTHDAY

Martin Waddell

"You know Biddy?" said McGlone. "It's her Birthday tomorrow."

"Good," said Buster.

"That'll mean a Party!" said Flash.

"No, it won't," said McGlone.

"Why not?" said Flash.

"Because Biddy's Mammy has no money, so there won't be any Birthday Party," said McGlone.

"Poor wee Biddy!" said Buster.

"Poor us!" said Flash, who liked Birthday Parties but didn't get to many, because there were only Buster and Flash and McGlone and Biddy at the End Cottages. McGlone always had a Party, and that was good, and Flash and Buster shared one, halfway between their real Birthdays, but that only made two, and Biddy's

Birthday should have made three Parties, but Biddy wasn't having one.

"You know us?" said McGlone.

"What about us?" said Buster.

"We could give Biddy a Birthday Party ourselves!" said McGlone.

They sat on the pier and thought about it.

"We haven't any money either," said Buster.

"You don't need money to give Birthday Parties," said McGlone.

"Biddy's Mammy thinks you do!" said Buster, sensibly.

"Mammies like to give *proper* Parties," said McGlone. "We're not Mammies, so we can give her our sort of Party!"

"Right!" said Buster.

"You're on!" whooped Flash.

"And I'll bash anybody who tells Biddy!" said McGlone, but she kept her glasses on, so Buster and Flash didn't take the threat seriously.

"Where'll we give it?" said Flash, bouncing about.

"Our wee house," said McGlone.

"We haven't got a wee house," said Buster. "Just the cottages."

"We can't give a party in the cottages, because of the Mammies," said McGlone. "That's why we're giving it in our wee house."

"*What* wee house?" objected Buster. "You

know we haven't got one!"

"We'll build one!" said McGlone.

"G–R–E–A–T!" yelled Flash.

That's why, when Biddy went looking for McGlone and Buster and Flash up and down the row, she couldn't find them. They weren't in the tide, swimming, and they weren't on the pier, fishing, and they weren't in the boats, mucking about, and they weren't in the back field, and they weren't up at the Castle. At least Biddy *thought* they weren't up at the Castle, but she couldn't be sure, because she wasn't allowed to go up to the Castle without McGlone to look after her, so she couldn't be certain, except that they weren't at the bit of the Castle she could see, standing on Kick-the-Ball's wall.

"They're not about, Mammy," she told her Mammy. "They've left me behind."

"McGlone wouldn't do that, Biddy," said Biddy's Mammy. "You know McGlone is very good. She always looks after you when I'm busy."

"So does Buster," said Biddy.

"Buster's good too, and Flash," said Biddy's Mammy. "They all look after you."

"They're fed up with my wee legs," said Biddy. "They're *always* saying it."

"What's wrong with your wee legs?" said her Mammy.

"Sometimes I won't walk on them," said Biddy.

"Why not?" asked her Mammy.

"Because my legs *are* wee, and they get tired before anybody else's," said Biddy.

"Well, you'd better go and practice walking on them, Biddy," said her Mammy. "Away off, because I've Something Special to do."

Biddy went out of the house, and had a practice walk all along the row, and a practice walk back, and there and back again, so she'd been four times the length of the row, but it didn't do her any good, because there was no sign of McGlone and Buster and Flash.

"No friends!" she told her Mammy.

"Just go and take another look for them, Biddy," said her Mammy, carefully keeping Biddy away from the kitchen door, so that she couldn't see what was on the table. "Take your wee legs for a walk. Then you can get wee-leg practice, and find McGlone."

So Biddy took her legs for a walk along the

tide, as far as Kick-the-Ball's broken boat, but she didn't find McGlone. She couldn't' go for a paddle, because she wasn't allowed to go for a paddle without McGlone, and she couldn't go and look in Baldy's hut in case they were hunting for eggs because she was scared of hens, and she couldn't go to the Castle because the Castle was out-of-bounds-too-dangerous-for-Biddy-on-her-own, and so she got fed up.

She went to *Mrs.* McGlone instead. She went in and sat on the potato sack.

"Don't say any rude words!" she told Mrs. McGlone.

"Like what?" said Mrs. McGlone.

"Like I'm not allowed to say it," said Biddy.

"I see," said Mrs. McGlone.

"McGlone did," said Biddy. "McGlone said it to Buster when he was sitting on the potatoes and McGlone was being Postmistress."

"She never did!" said Mrs. McGlone.

"She did, but I'm not," said Biddy. "I don't say rude words."

"Good," said Mrs. McGlone.

"Where's McGlone?" asked Biddy.

"I don't know," said Mrs. McGlone.

"I'm fed up with these legs," said Biddy, looking at them.

"They look nice legs to me," said Mrs. McGlone.

"They're *wee*," said Biddy.

"They'll get bigger," said Mrs. McGlone.

"When?" said Biddy.

"A bit bigger every day, Biddy!" said Mrs. McGlone.

"A *bigger* bit bigger tomorrow?" asked Biddy, hopefully.

"Why tomorrow?" asked Mrs. McGlone.

"Because tomorrow is my Birthday!" said

Biddy, and she went off to tell Kick-the-Ball about it, in case he knew where McGlone was.

"I haven't a baldy, Biddy!" said Kick-the-Ball.

"What's a baldy?" said Biddy. "Is it like Baldy Hagen, with no hair?"

"No," said Kick-the-Ball. "*I haven't a baldy* is a way of saying *I don't know*."

"You're not much use, are you?" said Biddy, and she went off.

Mrs. Cafferty was taking Wheezy his soup when Biddy found her.

"Why are you taking Wheezy his soup?" Biddy asked.

"Because his leg is broke," said Mrs. Cafferty.

"Does he make soup with his leg?" asked Biddy.

"He puts soup in him to fill up his leg, Biddy," said Mrs. Cafferty. "That makes his leg better."

"Is that why your legs are all old, Mrs. Cafferty?" said Biddy. "Or is that just your tights?"

"It's just my tights, Biddy," said Mrs. Cafferty, and she hitched her tights up, so they didn't sag around her ankles the way they usually did.

"Now you'll get yourself a man," said Biddy.

"I don't want a man, Biddy," said Mrs. Cafferty. "I had one, and I don't want another one! Women are best!"

"Like McGlone?" said Biddy.

"Exactly like McGlone," said Mrs. Cafferty, but she didn't know where McGlone was, when Biddy asked her.

Biddy went back to her house.

"What happened to Mrs. Cafferty's man, Mammy?" she said.

"Mr. Cafferty died, Biddy," Biddy's Mammy said.

"Well, she doesn't want another one," said Biddy.

"She must be very choosy," said Biddy's Mammy.

"I want some soup," said Biddy.

"What for?" said her Mammy, carefully closing the kitchen door again.

"To fill up my wee legs for my Birthday and make them big!" said Biddy.

"That'll do for our tea then, for we haven't anything else!" said her Mammy.

"Why haven't we anything else?" said Biddy.

"Because I've spent all the Benefit money," said her Mammy. "All there was of it, which wasn't much."

"What about the cleaning-caravans money?" Biddy asked.

"Shush now," said Biddy's Mammy. "There isn't supposed to be any cleaning-caravans money. Don't let the Welfare Man hear you."

"He isn't here," said Biddy.

"It's just as well!" said her Mammy.

"Am I getting soup?" said Biddy.

And she got it, but she didn't get it in the kitchen. Her Mammy brought it out to her, and never let her through the kitchen door, for she didn't want Biddy seeing what was in there.

The next morning McGlone came around for Biddy early, after she'd finished doing Baldy's hens.

"Happy Birthday, Biddy!" she said, and she gave Biddy a parcel.

It was a very small parcel.

There was a yellow gobstopper in it.

"T-h-a-n-k-o-v-e-r-m-u-c-h!" said Biddy, with the yellow gobstopper in her mouth which stopped her saying "Thank you very much," which was what she wanted to say.

They went down on the shore, and Buster came up.

"Happy Birthday, Biddy," he said, and he gave Biddy a parcel.

It was a very small parcel, done up in red paper, with a ribbon on it. It took Buster ages tying the ribbon.

There was a red gobstopper in it.

"T-h-a-n-k-o-v-e-r-m-u-c-h," said Biddy, putting the second gobstopper in on top of the first one.

Then Flash came up, and gave Biddy a paper bag with "FOR BIDDY FROM FLASH" on it.

"Is there another gobstopper in it?" Biddy said.

"Yes," said Flash.

"Thank you very much," said Biddy, properly this time, because she'd finished the first two gobstoppers. She put the third in her pocket for later. It was pink.

> *"Happy Birthday to you!*
> *You belong in a Zoo,*
> *With the monkeys, and the donkeys,*
> *And the big kangerooooo!"*

sang all the Gang.

"Is that all?" said Biddy.

"All what?" said McGlone.

"All I'm getting for my Birthday?" said Biddy.

"NO!" said McGlone.

"What else am I getting then?" said Biddy. "Where is it?" And she looked all around, but she couldn't see any more presents.

"Close your eyes and come with us, and you'll see!" said McGlone.

Biddy closed her eyes, and McGlone and Buster and Flash took her around the back of Kick-the-Ball's house and up to the Castle, and then McGlone said: "You can open your eyes now, Biddy!"

Biddy opened her eyes.

"What is it?" she said, looking at the pile of old driftwood and fish boxes and tires from the sea that was set against the far side of the Castle wall.

"It's your Birthday House!" said McGlone.

"Is it?" said Biddy.

"Me and McGlone made it!" said Flash.

"And me," said Buster.

"Look inside," said McGlone.

Biddy went inside.

"It's brilliant!" she said.

Then they all got inside the Birthday House, and McGlone showed Biddy where the cupboard

was, and the bed, and the chairs and the table.

"It's a great house!" said Biddy.

"We built it!" boasted Flash.

"McGlone got the tires," said Buster. "And Flash got the boards, and I got the fishboxes."

"And I got the cups and saucers," said McGlone.

She had the cups and saucers on the table, and she took the bottle of lemonade from the cupboard with the biscuits. They all came from the Shop That Never Shuts, after McGlone told her Mammy about making the Birthday House for Biddy.

Then Biddy ate her biscuits and she got up . . . just about, because there wasn't much room in the Birthday House . . . and she looked at her legs.

"Are they any bigger?" she asked McGlone,

"Not much," said McGlone.

"I thought they would be bigger," said Biddy.

"I'm sure you will get bigger, Biddy," said Buster.

"I thought I'd get bigger on my Birthday," said Biddy. "For there's nothing else."

"What do you mean nothing else?" said McGlone.

"My Mammy hadn't any money to get me anything," explained Biddy.

Then . . .

"BIDDY! BIDDY! B-I-D-D-Y!" somebody shouted.

"That's my Mammy!" said Biddy.

There was Biddy's Mammy coming up the path to the Castle, with a Great Big Birthday Cake with candles. And behind her was Kick-the-Ball with a parcel, and Baldy Hagen with a parcel, and Mrs. Cook with a parcel, and Mrs. Cafferty with three parcels, one from herself, and one from Wheezy Roberts, who couldn't get out of bed because of his broken leg, and another from Mrs. McGlone, who had to stay behind in the Shop That Never Shuts, and couldn't get to Biddy's Birthday in the Birthday House.

"P-R-E-S-E-N-T-S!" said Biddy.

And she opened them all.

There were beads from Kick-the-Ball and sweeties from Baldy and hankies from Mrs. Cook and a snowstorm from Mrs. Cafferty and a packet of crayons from Wheezy and a stick of rock from Mrs. McGlone.

"All for me!" said Biddy.

"And there's one more, Biddy!" said Biddy's Mammy. "A Big Surprise from me and all the neighbors!"

"It was McGlone's idea!" said Buster.

"Get it, McGlone!" said Biddy's Mammy.

And McGlone went off into the bushes, and came back with the Big Surprise.

It barked at Biddy!

It only made a wee tiny bark, because the Big Surprise was a wee tiny dog, but it had a collar on, and a little flappy tail that it flapped at Biddy.

"Mrs. Cafferty's puppy," said McGlone. "The brown-and-white one you said you wanted!"

McGlone put Mrs. Cafferty's puppy down in front of Biddy, and it wobbled around her, and licked Biddy's knee.

"Look at its wee eyes!" said McGlone.

"Look at its wee legs!" said Biddy.

"Just like yours," said Biddy's Mammy.

"So it will always be along with you if the others forget and leave you behind."

"It'll grow," said Biddy. "It will grow big legs."

"So will you!" said Buster.

Then McGlone put a bit of string through the Big Surprise's collar, and Biddy and McGlone and Flash and Buster walked it.

"I'm going to call it Josephine!" Biddy said. Josephine stopped walking, and whimpered, and whimpered, and sat down and looked at Biddy.

"It's your wee legs are the trouble!" Biddy told Josephine, and she bent down and picked the puppy up and carried her all the way back to the bed Biddy's Mammy had made for her in an egg box in front of the fire in Biddy's house.

McGlone and Buster and Flash and Biddy sat and watched, until Josephine stopped chewing the egg box, and went to sleep.

"I wish we had a dog," said Flash.

"Well, we haven't," said Buster.

"You can all share mine!" said Biddy.

"You're a great girl, Biddy!" said McGlone.

"You know what?" said Biddy.

"What?" said McGlone.

"This is the Best Birthday Ever!" said Biddy.

And the McGlone Gang agreed that she'd got it right!

THE FOX
AND THE
HEDGEHOG

Michael Scott

Sionnach the fox looked up suddenly, his pointed ears twitching, his wet black nose wrinkling. Something was coming. He lay flat on the ground and his brown coat so matched the piles of golden fallen leaves that it was impossible to see him. His nose wrinkled again, testing the damp forest air, sorting out the different forest smells: the wet ground, the rotting leaves and the sap of the different trees. He recognized the smell of the birds and the insects, faint and in the distance, he caught the hated smell of smoke, the sign of man. But it was the final and different odor that he couldn't make out. It was a musty, musky, dry sort of smell, and yet it also smelled damp and earthy.

Something rattled through some dry leaves

and Sionnach froze. He felt his heart beginning to beat and he had the sudden urge to sneeze—but that always happened at times like this.

More leaves rustled and then what looked like a small walking ball of leaves stopped right in front of the fox's hiding place. For a moment Sionnach didn't know what it was, but then he suddenly recognized it—it was a hedgehog.

Dinner, Sionnach thought, and he leaped out in front of the hedgehog.

Gráinne squealed with fright, and then she rolled herself up into a spiny ball. What a stupid fox, she thought.

Sionnach looked at the ball of spines in front of him and had second thoughts. Perhaps it had not been such a good idea just to jump out in front of the hedgehog like this. But he decided to do the best he could. "Well, I have you now," he said, grinning.

"Have you?" Gráinne asked, her voice sounding muffled because her head was tucked down and into her body.

Sionnach padded around the ball and tapped it with his paw. *Ouch!* Those spines hurt! What was he going to do with the hedgehog?

"What are you going to do with me?" Gráinne asked, almost as if she could read his mind.

"Well, I'm going to eat you of course," Sionnach said.

"How?" she asked.

But Sionnach didn't answer, because he wasn't too sure himself.

After a while, Gráinne said, "Why don't you let me go—I'm sure there will be something tastier along in a little while."

But Sionnach stubbornly shook his head. "No, I'm not going to let you go. I'm going to eat you."

"You will hurt yourself," Gráinne said, with what sounded like a sigh.

The fox looked at the spines and thought again. He had once run into a thorn bush when he was being chased by a pack of dogs, and he still remembered how sharp those thorns had been. Eating the hedgehog would be like chewing a thorn bush.

"Why can't you let me go?" Gráinne asked.

Sionnach shook his head again. "What would happen if the other foxes heard about it?" he asked. "They would only laugh at me, and say I couldn't even eat a simple hedgehog. I have my reputation to think of," he added proudly.

"A lot of foxes won't eat hedgehogs," she said after a while, "not unless they're very hungry. Are you very hungry?"

"Well not very. But I wouldn't mind some dinner now."

"Well, I'm terribly sorry, but I am not on the menu for today. Now I can lie here all day, and all night too, but you'll have to leave. So, you're just wasting your time."

Sionnach sat back on his haunches and looked at the spiky ball in front of him. If he turned her over he might be able to . . . but no, he shook his head. To do that would mean either using his paws, or his nose, and he didn't want to get either of those spiked. So, what he would have to do would be to trick the lady hedgehog. He closed his eyes and wondered just what he would do.

Time passed, and the sun moved slowly across the heavens, sending slanting beams through the branches. The autumn leaves turned bright red and gold, orange and bronze in the light, and it gave everything a rich, warm glow. Two of the last butterflies of summer chased each other through the trees, the sun turning their red and black wings to brilliant spots of color. They twisted around, darting and turning, resting for a few seconds on the warm branches of the trees before darting off again.

Sionnach watched them, their beautiful shapes and colors distracting him from the still curled-up hedgehog on the ground before his two front paws. And then he had an idea. He gave a short, sharp bark with excitement.

"I've had an idea," he said.

There was no movement or sound from the hedgehog—well almost no sound. The fox's sharp ears caught a low buzzing sort of sound, and it seemed to be coming from the hedgehog. He turned his head and brought his sharp ears down close to the small bundle . . . and found that it was snoring!

"Wake up," he barked.

"I'm awake, I'm awake," Gráinne grumbled. "What's wrong with you now?"

"I've had an idea," Sionnach said.

"So?"

"I'm going to let you go," the fox said quickly.

"Well I don't believe you," Gráinne said, just as quickly. "It's a trick or a trap."

"Why would I do that?" Sionnach asked in his most innocent voice.

"Because you're hungry and you want to eat me," the hedgehog said.

"Well . . ." the fox began.

"Well what?" Gráinne demanded.

"Well, I'm going to let you go. I am going to count up to one hundred and then I'm going to come after you. If I catch you, then I'll eat you; but if you reach the river before I catch you then I'll let you go."

"How do I know I can trust you?" Gráinne asked.

Sionnach looked hurt. "Because I'm a fox, and while we may be tricky and maybe we sometimes don't tell the full truth, we never tell lies."

"So, if I can reach the river, then I'm safe?" Gráinne asked.

Sionnach nodded. "That's right."

"And you'll count to a hundred first—all the way to a hundred?"

"All the way," he promised.

"When do we start?" she asked.

"As soon as you wish," he said.

Suddenly the hedgehog was up and running —well, waddling really—as quickly as she could into the forest. She was so quick that the fox was not quite ready, and she was already dis-

appearing along a winding track before he started counting.

"One . . . two . . . three . . . four. One . . . two . . . three . . . four."

Foxes can only count to four — one for each paw. So Sionnach did a quick sum and divided four into one hundred and came up with twenty-five. He began to scratch little marks in the ground with his nails for every "one, two, three, four." When he had twenty-five scratches he would go after the hedgehog.

Meanwhile, Gráinne had no sooner lost sight of the fox when she stopped and crept into the thickest thorn bush she could find and quickly wormed her way into its very center. She knew that she could not outrun the quicker fox, and she knew that he would be able to follow her scent there, but what she was hoping was that he would not be able to get in, and would eventually get tired and go away. Once she was in the very heart of the bush, she gave a huge sigh of relief.

"Is something the matter?" a thin, high voice asked above her head.

Gráinne looked up to find a sparrow peering down through the branches.

"A fox is after me," Gráinne said, and quickly told the sparrow what had happened. "Oh, I know that fox," said the sparrow—whose name was Gealbhan—"and once he finds out you're in here, he will sit outside for days and days. He doesn't give up easily."

"But I've got to get home to my little ones," Gráinne said, "I can't sit here for days. What am I going to do?"

Gealbhan cocked his small head to one side for a few minutes and then said, "Do you know of any other hedgehog living near the river?"

"Well there is my sister, Gráinneog," Gráinne said. "She lives in a tree stump right on the riverbank. That was where I was going when the fox stopped me."

"Well then," Gealbhan said, "here's what we'll do then . . ."

"ONE, TWO, THREE, four. One, two, three,

four." Sionnach took a deep breath and said as quickly as he could, "One, two, three, four. Here I come!"

The fox dashed down along the path, his long, low body weaving through the trees and bushes, his bushy tail flowing out behind him. At first he could catch faint traces of hedgehog scent, but after a while all traces of it disappeared. He began to get a little worried when there was neither sight nor smell of the creature, but he soon began to pick up the damp smell of the river, and he decided he would go there before turning back to check and see if she had decided to hide along the track. He was quite sure he was going to catch her, because of course, there was no way such a small, slow creature could outrun him, Sionnach the fox.

The fox ran out of the bushes and skidded to a halt in the soft ground of the riverbank. He stopped—right in front of a hedgehog. "What took you so long?" she asked, and curled up in a tight ball.

Sionnach looked at her in amazement for long moments before silently trotting away, shaking his head. He never did work out just how the hedgehog had beaten him to the river-bank, and he never tried to eat a hedgehog again.

JACK O'LANTERN

Retold by James Riordan

There was once a tinker of Ballingarry, down in County Limerick. As you are bound to know, all tinkers are as poor as fieldmice. So it was with Jack the tinker. Though, 'tis true, he was not as poor as he was humble, for he had a cottage to himself without a landlord, and a small garden behind with a fine apple tree. For a good part of the year Jack traveled the country, leaving his wife to mind the cottage and the garden.

One day while on his travels, Jack met a wayfarer and hailed him politely.

The wayfarer took a liking to the happy tinker and said to him, "I can grant you three wishes. Do the best you can with them, for such a chance will never come your way again."

Jack set to thinking hard and said, "Now that

you mention it, for sure I've an old armchair back home. Every visitor I have sits down in that armchair and makes me stand. So I wish that whoever sits in that chair shall stick there till I give the word."

"Granted," said the stranger. "Now let's hear your second wish, and I'd have you know to ask for something useful this time."

Jack fell to thinking once again, then said, "I've a tree in my garden that bears fine apples. But all the scalliwags for miles around steal every apple off that tree. So I wish that whoever goes to steal an apple will stick to that tree until I give the word."

"Granted," said the stranger. "Now, listen well, this is your last chance. Think of something really useful and say your piece."

Jack thought and thought, then smiled and said, "I know. My wife has a leather woolbag in which she keeps all her scraps of wool, and odds and ends besides. But little hooligans come to my house and tip all the wool upon the floor. I wish everything in that bag would stay there till I give the word."

"Granted," said the man. "But, my dear fellow, you've done not a scrap of good by yourself."

With that he went on his way shaking his head, while Jack the tinker turned for home as poor and carefree as before.

Some time after Jack's return, he slipped and fell and broke his leg, so he had to lie at home in bed the whole year through, unable to earn a living. His poor family were near starvation's door when a stranger chanced to pass their cottage and entered unannounced.

"I observe," the stranger said to Jack, "that your family's in great need. You are all starving, that's clear enough. Now I'm willing to strike a bargain with you: come to me at the end of seven years and I'll see you live in comfort until then."

"But who are you?" Jack inquired.

"Who am I?" echoed the stranger. "I'll tell you straight enough—I'm the Devil!"

"What matter?" murmured Jack, looking at his starving children. "I'll take your offer soon enough." And Jack gave his word to be ready at the end of seven years.

The Devil went on his way, leaving Jack as prosperous as a tinker ever has been. Henceforth there was never any lack of food within the house. No more did Jack go a'tinkering from place to place, or even if he did, it was more for pleasure's sake. Nor did his wife need to go a'woolpicking for her neighbors; she stayed at home, and all went well for the tinker and his wife, to the amazement of all the folks from around about.

In no time at all, the Devil went clean out of Jack's busy mind. Seven years passed by in bliss and comfort, but when the last day of the last year came around, Jack had a visitor.

"Your seven years are up," the Devil said. "I've kept my side of the bargain, now you keep yours."

"Sure enough," said Jack. "It's off I'll be with you in just a jiffy. Give me a moment to say farewell to my dear wife. In the meantime, just you sit here in my armchair and wait for me. I'll not be long."

The Devil sat himself down in Jack's armchair and waited. Since Jack had known his wife for going on twenty years, it didn't take him long to say good-bye. So he was soon back before the Devil.

"Come on," he said, "let's be going."

The Devil made to rise but, pull and jerk as he might, he could not budge from out the chair. He let out a string of curses that were heard across three townlands, and struggled fiercely. But it was no use. Seeing that he was stuck fast, he appealed to Jack.

"I'll grant you another seven years and twice as many riches if you will let me go."

"That's fair enough," said Jack. "Up and be away with you—back to where you belong."

The Devil was gone like a flash of lightning. Now Jack the tinker was doubly wealthy and his family lived in peace and comfort. But the seven years seemed to go twice as fast as before, for now Jack had twice as much to spend. Soon his time was up again and the Devil was at his door.

"I'll have none of your shenanigans this time, my lad," said the Devil. "Come on, let's go straightaway."

Jack made ready quickly, but said, as he left the house, "Let's make our way through my garden. Since I won't see it again, I'd like a last look at my apple-tree."

The Devil consented, and they walked together to the bottom of the garden and stood beneath the apple-tree, now overloaded with juicy apples.

"The day is warm," said Jack, "shall we not

take some apples with us to eat on the way? You are taller than I am—be so good as to pick us a couple of big'uns."

"I will do that same," the Devil said. And springing up he caught a large red apple, yet could not pull it off, nor let go of it. He stuck there swinging to and fro. He tugged and pulled, but it was no use.

Letting fly a curse that this time was heard from Galway down to Killarney, he shouted at Jack, "I'll grant you another seven years and thrice the wealth you had at first. Just let me down from out this tree."

Jack freed the Devil and off he raced without delay.

Now Jack and his family lived in wealth and plenty for seven more years. But just as autumn follows summer, and bad luck good, so at last the time was up and the Devil stood once more before him.

"To be sure now I'll stand none of your hanky-panky. And when I get you down in hell I'll make you pay for what you've done to me," he said to Jack.

Jack bid farewell to his wife, took down the leather woolbag from the wall and went off with the Devil.

They walked some way in silence, and then Jack said, "Do you know I had some fun when I was still a lad. I used to jump in and out of this old woolbag. Mind you, I was quick and nimble then."

"Any fool could do that," said the Devil with a grin.

"Go on, I bet you couldn't do it," retorted Jack. "You're too big and clumsy."

Jack held the woolbag open, and the Devil

sprang right in. In an instant the bag was shut with the Devil firmly trapped inside. How that Devil howled and screamed! But Jack would not listen. He marched over the hills with his bag on one shoulder until he came to a cornfield. There he saw three strong men threshing grain with wooden flails.

"Hey, boyoes," shouted Jack. "I've a bag here that's stiff and heavy. Will you give it a thrashing for me, to limber it up like?"

The men gladly walloped the bag, but so heavy was it that it broke their flails.

"Be off with you and that bag of yours," they cried. "The Devil himself must be in it."

"Oh, maybe it's himself that's in it, right enough," said Jack with a chuckle.

He walked on with the bag over his shoulder until he came to a water mill.

Going up to the miller, he said, "I want to soften this bag a little. Will you let it through your mill?"

The man agreed and Jack threw his bag into the mill. The miller was a mite surprised to hear a cracking and a smashing coming from the bag. He was even more astonished, and not a little cross, when his mill broke down.

"Get away with you," he shouted. "What's

that you've got in your bag, the Devil begorrah?"

"Sure and maybe it's the truth you're telling," said Jack, picking up his bag and walking off with it.

Presently, Jack came to a blacksmith's forge where six sturdy men were hammering at a piece of iron.

"Top of the morning to you, boys," called Jack. "What do you say to giving this old bag of mine a few hard whacks? It's that stiff and weighty!"

"Why now should we not?" said they.

The six men took their hammers and laid about the bag. With each blow it flew up in the air; this so enraged the men that they hammered even harder until they were tired and panting.

"Phew, the Devil himself must be in that bag," they railed at Jack.

One strong smith then lost his temper, seized a red hot iron from the fire and thrust it through the bag, catching the Devil unawares, so that he could not sit down for a whole year afterward!

The Devil howled and screamed, "Let me out. Let me out. I'll leave you in peace for good and give you riches four times over. Just leave me be."

At last Jack opened up the woolbag and let the Devil out. Away he shot as fast as his battered legs would carry him. Jack went back home and lived in plenty with his family for many a long year. But when he was very, very old, he felt just about ready to make his weary way to the other world. So off he went and stood before the gates of the good place. He knocked politely.

"Go away," came a voice. "Go back to the one you have worked for all your life. You can't come in here."

So Jack the tinker went and knocked on the gates of the bad place.

"Who's there?" came a voice.

"Jack the tinker from Ballingarry," Jack said.

"Don't let him in!" screamed a frightened voice. "He beat me black and blue and scorched my seat so badly I couldn't sit down for a month of Sundays!"

They would not let him in the bad place so back Jack went to the other place. They would not let him into heaven, so Jack was condemned to travel the world, always in the dark, and carrying only a small lantern.

He was to have no rest, but wander over bogs, swamps, moors and lonely places, leading folk astray. So Jack the tinker roams still, forever traveling the road until the Day of Judgment.

Folk know him now as Jack O'Lantern.

LAST BUS FOR CHRISTMAS

Patricia Lynch

"Hurry up there Miheal! Will ye bring over two red candles quick!"

"More strawberry jam, Miheal! Two one-pound jars! And raisins: four one-pound bags!"

"Miheal Daly! I'm wore out wid waitin' for twine. How can I parcel the customers' groceries wid ne'er an inch of string?"

Miheal grabbed a handful of string from the box in the corner behind the biscuit tins and ran with it to Mr. Coughlan. He brought the jam and the raisins at the same time to Peter Cadogan, and rolled the candles along the counter to Jim Rearden. Then he went back to his job of filling half-pound bags with sugar.

Miheal was the shop-boy and, one day, if he worked hard and behaved himself, Mr. Coughlan had promised to make him an assistant.

"There's grandeur for an orphan!" Mrs. Coughlan told him. "You should be grateful."

Miheal was grateful. But as he watched the women crowding the other side of the counter, filling market bags and baskets with Christmas shopping, he was discontented. Yet he had whistled and sung as he put up the colored paper chains and decorated the windows with yards of tinsel and artificial holly.

He nibbled a raisin and gazed out at the sleet drifting past the open door.

Everybody's going home for Christmas but me, he thought.

The Coughlans always went to their relations for Christmas. Mrs. Coughlan always left Miheal plenty to eat and Mr. Coughlan gave Miheal a shilling to spend. But Miheal never ate his Christmas dinner until they came back. After Mass he spent Christmas Day walking about the streets, listening to the noise and the clatter that came from the houses.

"Only two more hours," whispered Peter Cadogan, as Miheal brought him bags of biscuits and half-pounds of rashers as fast as Mr. Coughlan could cut them.

"Two more sugars, Miheal," said Jim Rearden. "Where d'you get your bus?"

Jim was new. He didn't know Miheal was an orphan, and Miheal was ashamed to tell him he had no home to go to for Christmas.

"Ashton's Quay," he muttered.

"We'll go together," said Jim over his shoulder. "I've me bag under the counter. Get yours!"

The next time Miheal brought Jim candles and raisins the new assistant wanted to know what time Miheal's bus went.

"I'll just make it if I run," said Miheal.

"Then get your bag, lad. Get your bag!"

Miheal slipped through the door leading to the house. He ran to his little dark room under the stairs. He didn't dare switch on the light. Mrs. Coughlan would want to know what he was doing. And a nice fool he'd look if she found out he was pretending to go home for Christmas.

"Home!" said Miheal to himself. "That's where a lad's people come from and mine came from Carrigasheen."

He wrapped his few belongings in a waterproof. He grabbed his overcoat from the hook behind the door and was back in the shop before Mr. Coughlan could miss him.

"Hi, Miheal! Give me a hand with this side of bacon. I never cut so many rashers in me life!"

Miheal pushed his bundle under the counter and ran to help.

"Isn't it grand to be going home for Christmas!" cried Peter, as they closed the door to prevent any more customers from coming in.

"Isn't it terrible to be turning money away!" groaned Mr. Coughlan.

But Mrs. Coughlan was waiting for him in her best hat and the coat with the fur collar.

"Can I trust you lads to bolt the shop door an' let yourselves out the side door?" demanded Mr. Coughlan.

"Indeed you can, sir!" replied Peter and Jim.

The last customer was served.

"I'm off!" cried Peter

"Safe home!" called the others.

Then Jim was running down the quay, Miheal stumbling after him, clasping his bundle, his unbuttoned coat flapping in the wind.

They went along Burgh Quay, pushing by the people waiting for the Bray bus, then down to Ashton's Quay.

"There's me bus!" shouted Jim.

"'Tis packed full!" murmured Miheal. He was terribly sorry for Jim. But maybe he would come back with him and they could spend Christmas together.

The bus was moving.

Jim gave a leap, the conductor caught his arm and pulled him to safety. He turned and waved to Miheal, his around red face laughing. He would have to stand all the way but Jim was used to standing.

Two queues still waited. Miheal joined the longest.

"Where are ye bound for, avic?" asked a stout countrywoman, with a thin little girl and four large bundles, who came up after him.

"Carrigasheen!" replied Miheal proudly.

"Ah well! I never heard tell of the place. But no doubt ye'll be welcome when ye get there. An' here's the bus."

"I'll help with the bundles, ma'am," said Miheal politely.

Now every seat was filled. Still more people squeezed into the bus. Miheal reached the step.

"One more an' one more only!" announced the conductor.

"In ye go ma'am!" said Miheal, stepping back.

The little girl was in. Miheal pushed the bundles after her and everyone cried out when the conductor tried to keep back the stout woman.

"Sure ye can't take the child away from her mammy!" declared a thin man. "Haven't ye any Christianity in your bones?"

"Can't she sit on me lap?" demanded the stout woman. "Give me a h'ist up, lad. And God reward ye!" she added, turning to Miheal.

He seized her under the arms. She caught the shining rail and Miheal gave a great heave.

He stood gazing after the bus.

"Now I'm stranded!" he said, forgetting he had no need to leave Dublin.

A dash of sleet in Miheal's face reminded him. He could go back to the lonely house behind the shop. His supper would be waiting on the table in the kitchen. He could poke up the fire and read his library book.

The quays were deserted. A tall garda strolled

along. He stared curiously at Miheal and his bundle.

"'Missed the bus, lad?" he asked.

"'Twas full up," explained Miheal.

"Bad luck!" sympathized the garda. "Can ye go back where ye came from?"

Miheal nodded.

"'Tis a bad night to be traveling!" said the garda. "That's the way to look at it."

He gave Miheal a friendly nod and passed on.

I'd as well be getting me supper, thought Miheal.

But he did not move.

Over the Metal Bridge came a queer old coach drawn by two horses. The driver was wrapped in a huge coat with many capes and a broad-rimmed hat was pulled down over his twinkling eyes.

He flourished a whip and pulled up beside Miheal.

The boy edged away. He didn't like the look of the coach at all.

The driver leaned over and managed to open the door at the side with his whip.

"In ye get! Last bus for Christmas!"

Whoever saw a bus with horses! thought Miheal. But I suppose they use any old traps at Christmas.

Still he held back.

"All the way to Carrigasheen widout stoppin'!" said the driver.

Miheal could see the cushioned seats and the floor spread thick with fresh hay. The wind, which was growing fiercer and colder every moment, blew in his face. He gave one look along the desolate quay and, putting his foot on the iron step, scrambled in.

At once the door slammed shut. The driver gave a shout and the horses trotted over the stones.

The coach bumped and swayed. Miheal tried to stretch out on the seat, but he slipped to the floor. The hay was thick and clean. He put his bundle under his head for a pillow and fell asleep.

An extra bump woke him up.

"I never thought to ask the fare," said Miheal to himself. "Seems a long way, so it does. Would he want ten shillings? He might—easy! Well, I haven't ten shillings. I've two new half-crowns. He'll get one and not a penny more!"

He tried to stand up, but the coach was

swaying from side to side and he had to sit down again.

"Mister! Mister!" he shouted. "How much is the fare?"

The rattle of the coach and the thunder of the horses' hooves made so much noise he could scarcely hear himself. Yet he could not keep quiet.

"I won't pay more than two and six," he shouted. "Mind now! I'm telling you."

The door of the coach swung open and Miheal was pitched out, his bundle following him. He landed on a bank covered with snow and lay there blinking.

The road wound away through the mountains in the moonlight—an empty desolate road. The wind had dropped but snow was falling.

In the distance he could hear a strange sound. It was coming nearer and nearer, and soon Miheal knew it was someone singing *Adeste Fidelis* in a queer cracked voice.

The singer approached, tramping slowly along: an old man with a heavy sack on his back.

"What ails ye to be sitting there in the snow, at this late hour of the night, young lad?" he asked, letting his sack slip to the ground.

"I came on the coach from Dublin," replied Miheal, standing up.

He was ashamed to say he had fallen out.

The old man pushed back his battered caubeen and scratched his head.

"But there hasn't been a coach on this road in mortal memory!" he declared. "There's the bus road the other side of the mountain and the last bus went by nigh on two hours ago. I suppose ye came by that. Where are you bound for?"

"Mebbe I did come by the bus and mebbe I didn't!" exclaimed Miheal. "But I'd be thankful if you'd tell me am I right for Carrigasheen?"

The old man wasn't a bit annoyed by Miheal's crossness.

"D'ye see the clump of trees where the road bends around by the mountain? There's Carrigasheen! I'm on me way there an' I'll be real glad of company. So ye're home for Christmas? I thought I knew everyone for miles around, yet I don't remember yer face. What name is on ye, lad?"

"Miheal Daly."

"There are no Dalys in Carrigasheen now. That I do know! But we can talk as we go. Me own name is Paudeen Caffrey."

Miheal caught up the sack. He was a strong lad but he found it heavy. He wondered how the old man had managed to carry it all. Paudeen Caffrey took the boy's bundle and they set off. The snow piled on their shoulders, on the loads they carried, on their hair, their eyebrows, but they did not notice, for Miheal was telling the old man all about himself.

"So me poor gossoon, ye're an orphan?" asked the old man.

"I am indeed!" agreed Miheal.

"An' ye haven't a father or mother, or brother or sister to be friend to ye?"

"Not a soul!"

"An' these people ye work for, what class of people are they?" continued old Paudeen Caffrey.

"Not too bad!" declared Miheal. "Aren't they going to make me an assistant one of these days?"

"Suppose now," began the old man. "Mind,

I'm just saying suppose—ye have a chance to be shop-boy to an old man and his wife that needed help bad in their shop and couldn't get it? Mind ye—I'm only supposing. Ye'd have a room wid two windas, one lookin' out on the market square, the other at the mountains. Ye'd have three good meals a day, a snack at supper, ten shillings a week, an' if you wanted to keep a dog or a cat, or a bicycle, ye'd be welcome. What would ye say to that?"

He looked at Miheal sideways and Miheal looked back.

"It wouldn't be with Paudeen Caffrey, that kept the corner shop next to the post office, would it?" asked Miheal.

"It would so," replied the old man.

"I'm remembering now," said the boy. "Me father told me if ever I needed a friend to write to Paudeen Caffrey."

"Why didn't ye, lad? Why didn't ye?"

"I was ashamed. My mother told me how they left Carrigasheen after telling everyone they were going to Dublin to make their fortunes an', when they came back, they'd be riding in their carriage. Ye see?"

The old man laughed.

"An' didn't ye come back in a carriage? But there's the lights of Carrigasheen. Do ye want to come home wid me, Miheal Daly?"

"If you'll have me, Mr. Caffrey."

The old man chuckled.

"An' to think I went out for a sack of praties an' come back wid a shop-boy! Wasn't it well ye caught the last bus for Christmas, Miheal?"

"It was indeed!" declared Miheal Daly.

He could see the corner shop with the door open and an old woman looking out. Beyond her he caught a glimpse of firelight dancing on the walls, of holy pictures framed in holly and a big red Christmas candle on the table waiting for the youngest in the house to light it.

TRAFFIC JAM

Frank Murphy

Dermot did not remember when trains ran on the line near his home. The rails had been taken away and there was only a wide grassy path where he went for a walk every day with his dog, Razor. Sometimes he sat on the bridge over the road and watched the roofs of cars, vans, and lorries disappear under his feet.

He was there one day, counting the vehicles which passed by. A loud rumble came from around the bend of the road, and a few moments later a monster yellow lorry came into view. It came slowly on. Dermot had never seen one as big. It slowed down and came to a halt just before the bridge. Dermot could imagine the driver looking at the sign which said, "Vehicles under 15 feet only." He must have been satisfied because the lorry moved on slowly.

The boy saw the bonnet vanish under his feet, then the cab, and finally the boxlike body of the lorry went slowly into the eye of the bridge. Then there was a frightening, grating sound of metal tearing against stone. The top of the lorry shivered and then the engine was switched off.

Razor barked in wild excitement and scuttled down the grass slope beside the bridge. Dermot followed at once. He went into the half dark under the bridge. The driver's head was out the window as he examined the roof of the lorry, jammed tight against the arch of the bridge. He muttered something under his breath and drew his head back inside the cab.

The engine started again. There was a whine as the back wheels of the lorry spun around at great speed, but the lorry did not move. Again and again the driver tried to back the lorry out of the bridge, but he failed each time. He got out and stood looking up at the top of the lorry, where it was jammed hard against the arch of the bridge. He moved to the other side, looked up again and scratched his head. He was puzzled.

Dermot spoke to him: "Sir, I know—"

"Ah, run away out of that, Sonny, and don't be bothering me," said the driver crossly.

"But, Sir—," Dermot began again.

"Go away! I tell you," growled the driver, and he sounded so angry that Dermot let him be.

Just then a horn sounded impatiently. A large black car had pulled up behind the lorry, and the driver was pressing on the horn. The lorry driver walked back to him.

"What's wrong?" asked the car driver.

"The lorry is stuck. I can't take it in or out," answered the lorry driver. The car driver got out, and he and the lorry driver went forward and stood looking up at the arch. The car driver looked so knowing that Dermot thought he must be an expert on cars stuck in bridges. He thought he heard him say that something "must be removed. There is no other way."

Other cars arrived and stopped, until a line of cars, lorries, and vans stretched from the bridge down the road and around the bend. Drivers and passengers got out and came to the bridge. It was a narrow bridge and the lorry was stuck at the center. No car could pass through.

After about ten minutes a large crowd had gathered. Most of the people just stood and looked, but five or six of them were speaking to the driver.

"The stones must be removed," said a tall dark man in a light raincoat.

"Nonsense," said a red-faced farmer in a floppy hat. "If you take away the stones of the arch, the whole bridge will fall down."

"The man is right," said a young man with fair hair. "There is only one way of getting it out. We must lower the roof of the lorry. Send for a sledgehammer and we'll batter it down."

"'Tis hard to know which of you is the silliest," said a van driver in a cloth cap. "How could you get at the part of the roof that's stuck? Isn't it under the bridge?"

"Then what would *you* do?" asked a lady in a fur coat.

"Me?" said the van driver.

"Yes, you!"

"There's only one way," said the van driver. "Dig a hole in the road behind the wheels and lower the lorry that way."

"I know a better way," shouted Dermot.

"The hole might work," said the farmer.

"I know a better way," shouted Dermot again.

"I thought I told you to go home, Sonny," said the lorry driver.

"Let the boy speak," said the woman in the fur coat. "His way couldn't be more stupid than some of yours. Speak up, boy!"

The people listened impatiently, because nobody expected Dermot to have a good idea. "Come on, boy. What have you to say?" said the van driver in the cloth cap.

"Let some of the air out of the wheels," said Dermot simply.

"What?" asked the lorry driver in surprise.

"Let some of the air out of the wheels," Dermot repeated.

"Ha-ha-ha haa," laughed the farmer. "The boy is right. His way is the answer."

The lorry driver rushed to one of the front wheels and knelt down. The people heard a loud hiss. He did the same at all the other wheels. They looked up. The roof of the lorry was no longer jammed against the arch of the bridge. The engine was started, and the huge yellow monster moved forward slowly on soft wheels. It passed out the other side and the crowd cheered.

Later Dermot sat on the bridge, watching the long line of traffic pass under his feet. He was happy because there was a fifty-pence piece in his pocket, given to him by the lorry driver.

POOR BANSHEE

Michael Killey

All by herself, in a crumbling tower on the wet, gray-green, crumbling moor, the banshee spent her gloomy days.

She never slept, but only wandered about like a bad shadow, combing her straggly, cobwebby hair with her spiky, scissory fingernails—and wailing, wailing, wailing like a strange bird. Black rings rimmed her sleepy eyes, and her face was as gray-green as the moor itself.

The banshee loved to wail.

She had learned many wailing songs from listening to the wind as it whined and whistled through the crumbling tower in winter.

It yowled and roared and yelped, as if in agony. Those were the songs that the banshee liked best. All winter through, the banshee would sit outside, with her feet in the heather, singing to herself.

But she was lonely with nothing except the wind to keep her company.

Poor banshee!

One day, the banshee wrapped a raggedy, threadbare cloak about her bony shoulders and left the crumbling tower behind. She went walking out across the moor. She was tired of sitting by herself.

After a time she came to a bare tree.

In the tree a crow was sitting, sighing now and then, and preening its black feathers. It looked as lonely as the banshee herself.

"Hello," said the banshee.

The crow looked down.

Its eyes opened wide.

It began to shiver.

Then it lifted itself up quickly—and flew away across the moor.

"Don't go!" cried the banshee. "I won't hurt you!"

Too late. The crow had gone.

"How odd," the banshee said.

The banshee came to a wall and crossed it. There was

a road there, winding into the distance. The banshee followed the road. As she walked, rain began to fall, washing the light from the ground.

By nightfall she came to a big, crooked house perched unsteadily on a crag above the moor. Inside, lights were being lit for the night.

The banshee hid behind a gate.

She began to sing.

She sang one of the wind's wildest songs.

Soon she heard noises from inside the house. Faces appeared at the window. The banshee was delighted. She sang more loudly than ever.

Voices began to cry out.

"It's the banshee! It's the banshee!" they shouted.

The faces turned whiter than the banshee's smock, and the shutters slammed tight, shutting in the light. The banshee could hear nothing but sobbing within.

She was puzzled.

What is wrong with me? she thought.

The banshee looked at herself in a puddle of rainwater.

"Am I so ugly?" she asked her reflection. "Is my face too gray-green? Is my hair too cobwebby?"

Far and wide the banshee wandered, wailing as she went. Hither and thither, thither and

hither she wound her way. She clambered over crags—and peered into dank, dripping caves—and crept on tiptoe through shadowy, black woods.

She looked under stones.

She sang for everyone she met.

Everywhere she went, it was the same. Everyone was afraid. They turned white at the sight of her. Her voice filled them with horror.

Poor, poor banshee!

At last, more lonely than ever, the banshee trudged back to her crumbling tower on the wet, gray-green, crumbling moor. She would never go out into the world again. People were so unfriendly.

As she went into her tower, the banshee heard something cry.

Was it the wind?

No, it was not the wind.

It was cats!

The cats had followed the banshee home. To and fro, from the crags to the crooked house; from the ruins to the black wood; and back again to the moor. They had heard the banshee wail and followed her dreadful cry.

The banshee was astonished to see so many cats.

Sixty-six cats had followed the banshee home: gray cats, white cats, lemon-and-orange cats, cats of silver and cats of gold.

The cats crept up to the banshee's door. They rubbed their scraggy heads against her shoes, they meowed sadly. They did not care what the banshee looked like. They only wanted supper.

Poor cats!

The banshee caught a potful of mice for the hungry cats, and made mouse stew. Then she fed it to them, one by one, in stone dishes. The cats gobbled it up greedily, every last bit.

Later, as night fell, the banshee sat out with her feet in the heather and the cats at her side—and she began to sing.

The cats did not run away.

They did not shiver, or open their eyes wide.

They did not even cry.

Instead they opened their mouths, and they too began to sing, screaking and shrieking like the wind itself. The air was torn to rags at the sound.

Poor banshee?

Not a bit of it!

The banshee was as happy as a banshee could be.

All together they spent their days, the banshee and her sixty-six cats, in the crumbling tower on the wet, gray-green, crumbling moor. She was lonely no longer and the cats had mouse stew for supper every night.

THE SELFISH GIANT

Oscar Wilde

Every afternoon, as they were coming from school, the children used to go and play in the Giant's garden.

It was a large lovely garden, with soft green grass. Here and there over the grass stood beautiful flowers like stars, and there were twelve peach-trees that in the spring-time broke out into delicate blossoms of pink and pearl, and in the autumn bore rich fruit. The birds sat on the trees and sang so sweetly that the children used to stop their games in order to listen to them. "How happy we are here!" they cried to each other.

One day the Giant came back. He had been to visit his friend the Cornish ogre, and had stayed with him for seven years. After the seven years were over he had said all that he had to say, for his conversation was limited, and he determined to return to his own castle. When he arrived he saw the children playing in the garden.

"What are you doing here?" he cried in a very gruff voice, and the children ran away.

"My own garden is my own garden," said the Giant; "anyone can understand that, and I will allow nobody to play in it but myself." So he built a high wall all around it, and put up a noticeboard.

He was a very selfish Giant.

The poor children had now nowhere to play. They tried to play on the road, but the road was very dusty and full of hard stones, and they did not like it. They used to wander around the high walls when their lessons were over, and talk about the beautiful garden inside. "How happy we were there!" they said to each other.

Then the Spring came, and all over the country there were little blossoms and little birds. Only in the garden of the Selfish Giant it was still winter. The birds did not care to sing in it as there were no children, and the trees forgot to blossom. Once a beautiful flower put its head out from the grass, but when it saw the noticeboard it was so sorry for the children that it slipped back into the ground again, and went off to sleep. The only people who were pleased were the Snow and the Frost. "Spring has forgotten this garden," they cried, "so we will live here all the year round." The Snow covered up the grass with her great white cloak, and the Frost painted all the trees silver. Then they invited the North Wind to stay with them, and he came. He was wrapped in furs, and he roared all day about the garden, and blew the chimney pots down. "This is a delightful spot," he said, "we must ask the Hail on a visit." So the Hail came. Every day for three hours he rattled on the roof of the castle till he broke

most of the slates, and then he ran around and around the garden as fast as he could go. He was dressed in gray, and his breath was like ice.

"I cannot understand why the Spring is so late in coming," said the Selfish Giant, as he sat at the window and looked out at his cold, white garden; "I hope there will be a change in the weather."

But the Spring never came, nor the Summer. The Autumn gave golden fruit to every garden, but to the Giant's garden she gave none. "He is too selfish," she said. So it was always winter there, and the North Wind and the Hail, and the Frost, and the Snow danced about through the trees.

One morning the Giant was lying awake in bed when he heard some lovely music. It sounded so sweet to his ears that he thought it must be the King's musicians passing by. It was really only a little linnet singing outside his window, but it was so long since he had heard a bird sing in his garden that it seemed to him to be the most beautiful music in the world. Then the Hail stopped dancing over his head, and the North Wind ceased roaring, and a delicious perfume came to him through the open casement. "I believe the Spring has come at last," said the Giant; and he jumped out of bed and looked out.

What did he see?

He saw a most wonderful sight. Through a little hole in the wall the children had crept in, and they were sitting in the branches of the trees. In every tree that he could see there was a little child. And the trees were so glad to have the children back again that they had covered themselves with blossoms, and were waving their arms gently above the children's heads. The birds were flying about and twittering with delight, and the flowers were looking up through the green grass and laughing. It was a lovely scene, only in one corner it was still winter. It was the farthest corner of the garden, and in it was standing a little boy. He was so small that he could not reach up to the branches of the tree, and he was wandering all around it, crying bitterly. The poor tree was still covered with frost and snow, and the North Wind was blowing and roaring above it. "Climb up! little boy," said the Tree, and it bent its branches down as low as it could; but the

boy was too tiny.

And the Giant's heart melted as he looked out. "How selfish I have been!" he said: "now I know why the Spring would not come here. I will put that poor little boy on the top of the tree, and then I will knock down the wall, and my garden shall be the children's playground for ever and ever." He was really very sorry for what he had done.

So he crept downstairs and opened the front door quite softly, and went out into the garden. But when the children saw him they were so frightened that they all ran away, and the garden became winter again. Only the little boy did not run for his eyes were so full of tears that he did not see the Giant coming. And the Giant stole up behind him and took him gently in his hand, and put him up into the tree. And the tree broke at once into blossom, and the birds came and sang on it, and the little boy stretched out his two arms and flung them around the Giant's neck, and kissed him. And the other children, when they saw that the Giant was not wicked any longer, came running back, and with them came the Spring. "It is your garden now, little children," said the Giant, and he took a great axe and knocked down the wall. And when the people were going to market at twelve o'clock they found the Giant playing with the children in the most beautiful garden they had ever seen.

All day long they played, and in the evening they came to the Giant to bid him good-bye.

"But where is your little companion?" he said: "the boy I put into the tree." The Giant

loved him the best because he had kissed him.

"We don't know," answered the children: "he has gone away."

"You must tell him to be sure and come tomorrow," said the Giant. But the children said that they did not know where he lived and had never seen him before; and the Giant felt very sad.

Every afternoon, when school was over, the children came and played with the Giant. But the little boy whom the Giant loved was never seen again. The Giant was very kind to all the children, yet he longed for his first little friend, and often spoke of him. "How I would like to see him!" he used to say.

Years went over, and the Giant grew very old

and feeble. He could not play about anymore, so he sat in a huge armchair, and watched the children at their games, and admired his garden. "I have many beautiful flowers," he said, "but the children are the most beautiful flowers of all."

One winter morning he looked out of his window as he was dressing. He did not hate the Winter now, for he knew that it was merely the Spring asleep, and that the flowers were resting.

Suddenly he rubbed his eyes in wonder and looked and looked. It certainly was a marvelous sight. In the farthest corner of the garden was a tree quite covered with lovely white blossoms. Its branches were golden, and silver fruit hung down from them, and underneath it stood the little boy he had loved.

Downstairs ran the Giant in great joy, and out into the garden. He hastened across the grass, and came near to the child. And when he came quite close his face grew red with anger, and he said, "Who hath dared to wound thee?" For on the palms of the child's hands were the prints of two nails, and the prints of two nails were on the little feet.

"Who hath dared to wound thee?" cried the Giant, "tell me, that I may take my big sword and slay him."

"Nay," answered the child: "but these are the wounds of Love."

"Who art thou?" said the Giant, and a strange awe fell on him, and he knelt before the little child.

And the child smiled on the Giant, and said to him, "You let me play once in your garden, today you shall come with me to my garden, which is Paradise."

And when the children ran in that afternoon, they found the Giant lying dead under the tree, all covered with white blossoms.

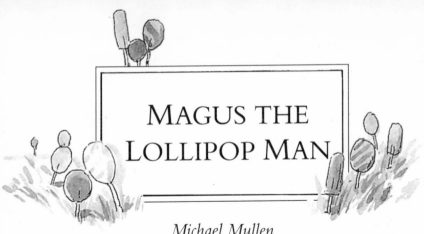

MAGUS THE LOLLIPOP MAN

Michael Mullen

Magus the lollipop man came down the hill and stood on the bridge one summer morning. From the bridge he could see the town of Hornbottom. The sun was pink and half hot. Its rays caught the dewdrops on the grass blades and filled them with silver. On the trees the leaves were full and green and cool. And the pink light was getting in everywhere. It floated over window sills and lit up all the dark corners of rooms. It was going to be a hot day but it was not as yet hot.

The lollipop man was a fat man. He had a large floppy hat and the wide brim cast a shadow on his eyes. He had a very large coat which was more like a cloak. It was twice too big for a man but for the lollipop man it was just right. It had foot-and-a-half deep pockets and they were all stuffed with lollipops.

He stood on the humped back bridge which had been built a long time ago and listened to the waters rush over the rocks a little upstream. It was a soft sound like a hush which wanted the world to listen. He listened. He could hear the song of the birds from the trees and the bushes and the shrubs. The sound was everywhere and it filled his ears.

Magus the lollipop man looked at the town. It was not a large town, just large enough for a lollipop man to set his lollipops before the children were awake in the green lawns which had been carefully cut until they looked like carpets. His lollipops were just a little taller than the cut grass and there they could shine in the sun. Lollipops were never planted in fields.

The village clock had a solemn face. It had been solemn for two hundred years and its twelve figures and two hands were very large. It was coming up to seven o'clock. The bells rang out. They rang out eight times for seven hours and the lollipop man knew that the vicar was a sensible man. Nobody else in the world had a clock which rang eight times when the small hand showed up at seven. He wondered if the bells rang once or thirteen times when the small hand reached twelve.

He milked his long white beard. He always milked his long white beard when he was deciding upon something. He had decided on where to begin planting lollipops. He made his way to the Yellow Tavern which had its blinds down like large eyelids. He plunged his hand deep into his pockets and took out a handful of lollipops. There were yellow lollipops and green lollipops and blue lollipops and red lollipops and many other colored lollipops.

"Aha," he said with a long "aah", "I will start planting lollipops here. I will plant all sorts of colored lollipops for Barney Perkins for something tells me, which tells me everything, that Barney Perkins is not just feeling himself at this very moment."

Barney Perkins had not been feeling himself

for a long time now and Mister and Missus Perkins were very worried about him. For no reason at all he had taken ill. He became very thin and Doctor Pink had poked at him and examined him and mused about him and could find nothing wrong with him. But that did no good for Barney Perkins. He wasted away in the big room above the tavern and Missus Perkins who was very fat and full was worried. He refused his breakfast and he refused his dinner and he refused everything which was brought to him and lots of things had been brought to him. He lay in his bed very weak, his head deep in large pillows and he only moved his large blue eyes.

· "Colored lollipops for Master Perkins," the lollipop man said, selecting lollipops from the handful of lollipops he held before him. He selected them carefully and put the rest of them back into his deep pockets. Then moving about the lawn briskly he planted a circle of colored lollipops with the initials BP in the middle, which stood for Barney Perkins, and went on his way.

He stopped by another garden and looked at the lawn. It was a sad, badly cut lawn and the grass was thick and tufted and falling to one side. He looked at the house. It certainly needed a new coat of paint and the pink sun cheered it up only a little. The paint on the door had blistered here and there and the weather board was held on one hinge so that it scraped every time the door was opened. Yes, the lollipop man knew all about it. "This is little George Wallace's house. He is the orphan who stays with Missus Tucker. Why, little George Wallace hasn't had a lollipop since way back before Christmas and Missus Tucker treats George very badly. Nobody likes George Wallace or his little dog."

He plunged his hand deep into his pocket and fetched out the very largest lollipop he had. It must have been as large as a dinner plate and thick as a thumb and it would require a whole

night and a whole day of tongue-licking just to wear it half thin. It was the best lollipop he had and it had taken him a whole week to mix its colors. He pushed the stem into the ground and then straightened his stiff back to look at it. It looked like the sun coming up out of the sea in the green grass which was falling to one side.

He bent down again, his old bones creaking and placed small lollipops around the large one. "Yes," he said to himself, "Little George Wallace will be pleased with his lollipops. Just wait until he sees them. Why, his face will just light up!" And having said that he was on his way again.

He made his way down the street, his large coat gathered about him and his large brimmed hat flopping over his ears and his eyes. The sun was getting warmer and the shadows thrown by the houses shorter. Summer sun is good for a lollipop man's back. It warms him up and dries out the dew which comes up at night from the ground when he is sleeping by the hedgerows.

He worked during the winter in his little cottage boiling sugars and mixing in colors and tastes from large bottles which he kept on his shelves. Nobody knew how to mix colors and tastes except a proper lollipop man. It was an old secret he had learned from an old lollipop man when he was very young. He had learned which berries to crush into juice in his press which was made with wood from the mast of a Spanish galleon he had found on the coast of Cornwall. Of course it took time to learn how to know good berries from bad ones and a wet summer with little sun always made him sad. He knew then that the juice would be poor and thin and the lollipops themselves without luster. Last year had been good for lollipops.

The milkman, Councillor Bitterberry, came by on his float and gave him a quizzical eye.

Strangers were never welcome in Hornbottom, particularly ones with deep pockets. One never knew what they were up to between stealing hens and vegetables and making off with eggs. The rattle of the wheels on the cobblestones made a racket which disturbed the quiet corners of the town.

Magus found more lawns and planted more lollipops. He looked about at his morning's work and a broad smile spread over his face. He had certainly brightened up the town. He felt very satisfied with himself. He turned and made his way down to the river. He would sleep there under the trees and listen to the water passing by and later in the day he would steep his tired feet. They were very sore and very red for he had walked a long way during the night and had only taken a short rest on the way. He always had to have his work finished very early in the morning. A lollipop man must never be caught growing lollipops. That was the first rule.

MUNACHAR
AND
MANACHAR

Retold by James Riordan

There once lived a Munachar and a Manachar a long time ago, and it is a long time since it was, and if they were alive now they would not be alive then.

They went out together to pick raspberries, and as many as Munachar used to pick Manachar used to eat. Munachar became so cross that he decided to look for a rod to make a beam from which to hang Manachar who ate his raspberries every one. And he found a rod.

"What news today?" asked the rod.

"It is my own news that I'm seeking," said Munachar. "I'm looking for a rod, a rod to make a beam from which to hang Manachar who ate my raspberries every one."

"You will not have me," said the rod, "until you get an axe to cut me."

So Munachar came to an axe.

"What news today?" asked the axe.

"It is my own news I'm seeking," replied Munachar. "I'm looking for an axe, an axe to cut a rod, the rod to make a beam, a beam from which to hang Manachar who ate my raspberries every one."

"You will not have me," said the axe, "until you get a whetstone to sharpen me."

He came to a whetstone.

"What news today?" asked the whetstone.

"It's my own news I'm seeking. I'm looking for a whetstone, a whetstone to sharpen an axe, the axe to cut a rod, the rod to make a beam, the beam to hang Manachar who ate my raspberries every one."

"You will not have me," says the whetstone, "until you bring water to wet me."

He came to the water.

"What news today?" asked the water.

"It's my own news that I'm seeking. I'm looking for water, water to wet a whetstone, the whetstone to sharpen an axe, the axe to cut a rod, the rod to make a beam, the beam to hang Manachar who ate my raspberries every one."

"You will not have me," said the water, "until you bring a deer who will swim me."

He came to a deer.

"What news today?" asked the deer.

"It's my own news I'm seeking. I'm looking for a deer, a deer to swim water, the water to wet a whetstone, the whetstone to sharpen an axe, the axe to cut a rod, the rod to make a beam, the beam to hang Manachar who ate my raspberries every one."

"You will not have me," said the deer, "until you bring a hound who will hunt me."

He came to a hound.

"What news today?" asked the hound.

"It's my own news I'm seeking. I'm looking for a hound, a hound to hunt a deer, the deer to swim water, the water to wet a whetstone, the whetstone to sharpen an axe, the axe to cut a rod, the rod to make a beam, the beam to hang

Manachar who ate my raspberries every one."

"You will not have me," said the hound, "until you get a bit of butter to put in my paw."

He came to the butter.

"What news today?" asked the butter.

"It's my own news I'm seeking. I'm looking for butter, butter to put in a hound's paw, the hound to hunt a deer, the deer to swim water, the water to wet a whetstone, the whetstone to sharpen an axe, the axe to cut a rod, the rod to make a beam, the beam to hang Manachar who ate my raspberries every one."

"You will not have me," said the butter, "until you bring a cat who will scrape me."

He came to a cat.

"What news today?" said the cat.

"It's my own news I'm seeking. I'm looking for a cat, a cat to scrape butter, the butter to put in a hound's paw, the hound to hunt a deer, the deer to swim water, the water to wet a whetstone, the whetstone to sharpen an axe, the axe to cut a rod, the rod to make a beam, the beam to hang Manachar who ate my raspberries every one."

"You will not have me," said the cat, "until you bring me milk."

He came to a cow.

"What news today?" asked the cow.

"It's my own news I'm seeking. I'm looking

for a cow, a cow to give me milk, the milk to give to a cat, the cat to scrape butter, the butter to put in a hound's paw, the hound to hunt a deer, the deer to swim water, the water to wet a whetstone, the whetstone to sharpen an axe, the axe to cut a rod, the rod to make a beam, the beam to hang Manachar who ate my raspberries every one."

"You will not have milk from me," said the cow, "until you bring me a whisp of straw from the threshers."

He came to the threshers.

"What news today?" asked the threshers.

"It's my own news I'm seeking. I'm looking for a whisp of straw, a whisp of straw to give to a cow, the cow to give me milk, the milk to give to a cat, the cat to scrape butter, the butter to put in a hound's paw, the hound to hunt a deer, the deer to swim water, the water to wet a whetstone, the whetstone to sharpen an axe, the axe to cut a rod, the rod to make a beam, the beam to hang Manachar who ate my raspberries every one."

"You will not have a whisp of straw from us," said the threshers, "until you bring us a cake from the miller."

He came to the miller.

"What news today?" asked the miller.

"It's my own news I'm seeking. I'm looking

for a cake, a cake to give to the threshers, the
threshers to give me a whisp of straw, the whisp
of straw to give to a cow, the cow to give me
milk, the milk to give to a cat, the cat to scrape
butter, the butter to put in a hound's paw, the
hound to hunt a deer, the deer to swim water,
the water to wet a whetstone, the whetstone to
sharpen an axe, the axe to cut a rod, the rod to
make a beam, the beam to hang Manachar who
ate my raspberries every one."

"You cannot have a cake from me," said the
miller, "until you bring me a full sieve of water
from the river."

Munachar took the sieve in his hand and went
down to the river, but when he put it in and out
of the water, the water ran out again; he would
never have filled it if he had been there
from that day to this. All of a sudden,
a crow went flying by.

"Daub, daub!" said the crow.

"My blessings on you," said
Munachar, "but it's the good
advice you have."

And he took some red clay
and daubed it on the bottom
of the sieve until all the holes
were filled; and then the sieve
held water, and he brought the
water to the miller, and the

miller gave him a cake, and he gave the cake to the threshers, and the threshers gave him a whisp of straw, and he gave the whisp of straw to the cow, and the cow gave him milk, the milk he gave to the cat, the cat scraped the butter, the butter went into the hound's paw, the hound hunted the deer, the deer swam the water, the water wet the whetstone, the whetstone sharpened the axe, the axe cut the rod, and the rod made the beam; and when he had it ready to hang Manachar . . . he found that Manachar had . . . BURST!

Acknowledgments

The publisher would like to thank the copyright holders for permission to reproduce the following copyright material:

Sigerson Clifford: Mercier Press for "The Four Magpies" by Sigerson Clifford from *The Red Haired Woman and Other Irish Stories* published by the Mercier Press, 5 French Church Street, Cork, Ireland; copyright © Sigerson Clifford. **Tony Hickey**: Peters Fraser & Dunlop Group Ltd. for "The Flying Display" from *Granny Wants to Fly* by Tony Hickey, Ginn & Company Ltd.; copyright © Tony Hickey 1993. **Eamon Kelly**: Poolbeg Press Ltd. for "Petie Flimin and the Whale" from *The Enchanted Cake* by Eamon Kelly, Poolbeg Press Ltd. 1992; copyright © Eamon Kelly 1992. **Michael Killey**: the author for "Poor Banshee"; copyright © Michael Killey 1995. **Patricia Lynch**: Eugene Lambert for "Last Bus for Christmas" from *Strangers at the Fair* by Patricia Lynch; copyright © Patricia Lynch 1945. **Michael Mullen**: Canongate Press Ltd. for the extract from *Magus the Lollipop Man* by Michael Mullen, Canongate Press Ltd. 1981; copyright © Michael Mullin 1981. **Frank Murphy**: The Educational Company of Ireland for "Traffic Jam" by Frank Murphy from *Links I*, The Educational Company of Ireland 1976 (a trading unit of Smurfit Services Ltd.) **Edna O'Brien**: Pavilion Books for "The Leprechaun" from *Tales for the Telling*, Pavilion Books 1986; copyright © Edna O'Brien 1986. **John O'Connor**: The Estate of John O'Connor for "Neilly and the Fir Tree" by John O'Connor. **Majorie Quarton**: Poolbeg Press Ltd. for "The Story of the First Greyhound" from *The Cow Watched the Battle* by Marjorie Quarton. Poolbeg Press Ltd. 1990; copyright © Marjorie Quarton 1990. **James Riordan**: Reed Consumer Books Ltd. for "Jack O'Lantern" from *A World of Folk Tales* by James Riordan, Hamlyn 1981; copyright © James Riordan 1981, and the author for "The Man with No Story", "Una and the Giant Cucullin" and "Munacher and Manacher"; copyright © James Riordan 1995. **Michael Scott**: Mercier Press for "The Fox and the Hedgehog" from *Irish Animal Tales* by Michael Scott published by the Mercier Press, 5 French Church Street, Cork, Ireland; copyright © Michael Scott 1989. **Martin Waddell**: Murray Pollinger Literary Agent for "Biddy's Birthday" from *Tales from the Shop That Never Shuts* by Martin Waddell, Viking Kestrel 1988; copyright © Martin Waddell 1988.

Every effort has been made to obtain permission from copyright holders. If any omissions have been made, we shall be pleased to make suitable corrections in any reprint.